Murder With a Sip of Eggnog

An Ivy Clark Mystery

Kristy T Dixon

For Velda Kay Chipman

Chapter 1

"It's too cold," I said, sitting on the window seat with Creepers on my lap. "All those years I wished for a white Christmas, I didn't realize how cold snow actually was. I only want snow once a year, then I need sun."

Creepers meowed and shifted positions. He didn't care about the weather. As long as he was fed and had a window, he was content.

Snow had fallen all night and was still going strong.

"Delivery!" Jett's voice called from the door. He'd come up from the diner. I had a private entrance, but the stairs were steep and currently covered in ice. Perks of living above the diner meant I might not have to go outside until spring.

"Come in," I called.

The door opened, and Jett entered. He had a large mug full of hot chocolate. "I thought you might be hibernating up here." He handed me the mug.

"You're the best."

"I try." He sat at the foot of my bed. "We got a ton of snow. No point in doing my rounds. The roads are too bad to get to the nearby towns."

"You can hibernate with us," I said. "Creepers isn't keeping up his side of the conversation again."

Creepers glared at me and jumped to the floor.

"I think I insulted him." I took a sip from my mug.

"Probably. Your mom called me last night."

I groaned. "Why? Do I want to know?"

"She wants me to bring you to Arizona for Christmas."

I grinned. "She wants me to leave this frozen wasteland and go to paradise?"

"Something like that."

"You can't leave work."

He tilted his head and smiled. "Sure I can. I have time saved up."

"Don't you need that for the wedding?"

"I have enough to take a week now and still have some left in January. Use it or lose it."

"Do you want to go?"

"I want to do whatever you want to do."

I moved my lips from side to side in thought. "We can't leave Boyd alone at Christmas."

"I told your mom you'd say that. She said there's room for Boyd."

My heart felt lighter. "I feel like I've adopted Boyd. I would love to visit my parents."

"Then let's go. I'll talk to Boyd. You call your mom and figure out the dates." He stood and stretched. "I can take a week. Any longer and this town might collapse."

"I think your deputies can handle it," I said, placing my mug on the window seat.

"They'd better."

I stood and wrapped my arms around him. "Will your parents be okay with you being gone for Christmas?"

Jett was the best. I knew he would sacrifice what he wanted for me, and I didn't want to ruin his holidays.

"Nope. They're going on a cruise. They get back the day after."

"Right. I forgot about that."

I ran my fingers through his brown hair and leaned in—

His phone rang. He kissed me lightly and answered, "Sheriff Malone... Hi, Opal. Mm-hmm."

I grabbed my mug and took another sip. If Opal was upset about something, it could be a long call. She liked to complain about everything. Whatever story she told went on and on and rarely had an ending in sight.

"Why would you try to drive in this? Okay, okay," he said. "I'll be right there." He slipped his phone into his pocket. "Opal tried to drive into town. She's stuck. I need to go dig her out."

I felt guilty I'd believed Opal was only calling to complain, but I worried about Jett.

"You'll get stuck too."

"I'll beg Hal at the hardware store to get his snowplow. I'll follow him."

"I didn't know Opal drove."

"She doesn't very often. She's never driven much, even when she was younger. I don't know why she decided to try it today. I'll grab someone to go with me. I'll talk to you later."

I watched him leave and sighed. I didn't even get a decent kiss, thanks to Opal. It was fine. Jett's lips were worth the wait.

I pictured Opal's old car in my mind, sitting unused and covered in dust in her garage. Why, of all days, did she choose today to change that?

Going to Arizona on short notice would take some work. Flights weren't easy to find this close to Christmas. I ran a brush through my blond hair and pulled it into a ponytail. I couldn't stay up here forever. Creepers was tired of me. I went to pet him, and he ran off.

I stepped into my shoes and went down to the diner. There wasn't anyone in the dining area except Livy, one of the servers.

"Good morning," I said.

Livy smiled. "It'd be better if I were curled up by a fireplace with a book."

"That does sound perfect. Are you the only server here?"

"Yep. José told the staff to stay home. Said he could manage the kitchen alone."

"I'll be shocked if anyone shows up," I said. "You can probably go home if you want. I can help if someone wanders in."

"Anton's coming by in an hour. If no one shows up, I'll leave with him."

José came out of the kitchen. "Hey, Ivy. I don't think anyone will come today. We could probably close, but then I'd feel bad if someone braved the elements to get here."

"Opal's stuck in a snowbank. I bet Jett brings her here once he digs her out."

"Why would she try to drive through this?"

"It's normally a Zumba day, but I canceled. Maybe she didn't get the text. I'm going to Arizona for the week of Christmas. Will that be a problem?"

"Nope," José said. "I have it covered."

"You can close any days you need to. No pressure."

"The weather is supposed to get better. I bet we can stay open every day but Christmas."

"When do the new cooks start?"

"I'll train one of them next week, and the other the week after."

We were finally going to have enough cooks to work real shifts. José, Anton, and Carrie had been working too much for too long.

With two more cooks, they could finally get a break. Carrie's sister Tiffany kept saying she wanted more hours, but so far, that hadn't translated into showing up.

"Is Jett going to Arizona with you?" Livy asked.

"Yes. And Boyd."

Livy giggled. "You're taking Boyd to your parents' house for Christmas?"

I shrugged. "He doesn't have anywhere else to go."

"Won't that be weird?"

"No. My mom knew Boyd when she grew up here."

"I forgot about that."

"He's like a grandpa to me. I'm not letting him spend the holidays alone."

The morning dragged by. No one came in the first hour. I stayed to keep Livy and José company. When Anton arrived, he stomped snow off his boots and said he just needed to warm up before heading back out.

The four of us sat at a booth, bundled up with mugs of hot chocolate and a plate of sugar cookies in the middle.

"What are your plans for Christmas?" I asked them.

Livy's eyes lit up, and she twisted a piece of red hair around her finger. "Anton's coming to my house in the morning, then we're visiting his family. In the evening, we're going to decorate gingerbread houses."

"That sounds fun. What about you, José?"

"First Christmas in a long time when I'm not alone," he said with a smile. "Carrie and I are staying home, watching movies, and eating too much."

José and Carrie had gotten married a few months ago. I was glad they wouldn't be lonely this year. José had been one of the first people to befriend me here, and I loved seeing him so happy.

"Although, to be fair, that's not wildly different from what we do every night. I've gained ten pounds since the wedding." He patted his flat stomach.

"Please," I said with a smile. "We all know that's a lie."

"Poor José," Anton said with mock sympathy. "At this rate, you'll be playing Santa by next week."

José gave him a playful kick under the table. "Hey. It's not easy staying fit when you and your wife both cook like professionals."

"Are you mocking my cooking?" Anton asked.

"No, no. You do a very tolerable job."

"Tolerable? What's that supposed to mean?"

"You're a great cook," Livy cut in. "Don't let José tease you."

José laughed. "He is. We wouldn't have hired him otherwise."

The door opened, and a blast of cold air followed Jett and Opal inside. Opal brushed snow from her gray hair and slumped into the nearest booth. They looked like they'd walked through a snow globe.

"Are you alright?" I asked, standing up.

She scowled. "Slightly frozen. The sheriff took his sweet time digging me out. What's the point of all those muscles if it takes him half a day to get my car out of a ditch?"

Jett just grinned and shook his head. "Is the hot chocolate maker working?"

"Yep," I said.

"I'll grab you some hot chocolate."

"That's the least you can do, Sheriff." She wiped her nose with a tissue and sighed.

Jett went into the kitchen, and José chuckled.

"It was nice of Jett to drop what he was doing to go dig you out," I said.

"I suppose."

"Why were you driving in this?"

"I hate getting snowed in at my house. It's too far from everything. I'd rather be snowed in at town. I'll get a room at the B&B."

"It'll be nice for you when your condo gets built. You'll always be in town."

"I'm looking forward to it."

Jett came out with a mug and handed it to Opal. She took a sip. "Too much powder."

We were all used to Opal. Her comments used to bother me, but then I realized it was just the way she was. Ignoring her comments was better than getting insulted by them.

"I need to go make a call," I said. "I'll be back."

I went upstairs to sit in the living room and called my mom.

"Hi, Ivy," she said. "Did Jett talk to you?"

"Yes. Why didn't you call me?"

"I've been trying to get you to come visit for a while. I figured I could guilt Jett into bringing you."

"Thanks, Mom. I'm going to look at tickets."

"Bring Boyd."

"I will."

"I'm dying to see your ring in person. And we can talk about wedding details."

"Sure. We aren't going to go crazy. There isn't a lot we need." I held out my hand and moved it under the light to watch my ring sparkle.

"I know you. If I don't help, you'll get married in the diner in an apron. We can't have that."

I smiled. "I have my eye on a dress. You don't have to worry."

"Is José going to make your cake?"

"I never thought about that, but I bet he could. Carrie's good at decorating things. She could probably help."

"I've been talking to Carol Malone at least once a week. She might be more excited than I am."

Jett's mom was great. She'd known my mom all her life, and they had a nice bond. "I hope you two aren't planning everything without us."

"We're not going to take over your big day. We're just excited. Have you warned Jett about Frank and Dad?"

"No, I forgot." Frank was my parents' neighbor across the street. Every year, my dad and Frank tried to outdo each other with their Christmas decorations. It had started as a joke, but it got worse and worse every year. It had gone from classy to trashy. My mom hated it. If there was a hideous Christmas decoration, my dad would buy it and stick it in the front yard.

"It might be better this year," my mom said. "The neighborhood is having a house decorating competition, but the houses in the competition have to make it look like a gingerbread house."

"That's fun."

"I told your dad that means he has to make it cute. Nothing tacky and nothing inflatable. There's almost no room in the garage with all his decorations."

"Has he started?"

"Yep. He's been working on it since Thanksgiving."

"How does it look?"

"Busy, but better than some years."

"How does Frank's look?"

"The same."

"I can't wait to see it."

"I wish he would stop. He says it's done, then he finds something else. He needs to get a second job to pay for this weird hobby."

"Is it that bad?"

She laughed. "No. I guess it's good he has something to do with his time. We can't wait to see you."

I smiled. I hadn't been home in over a year. It was time.

Chapter 2

My parents' house looked amazing. We pulled up in our rental car and stared at the gingerbread decorations. Huge candy canes stood on both sides of the door, and two-foot-high gumdrops lined the edges of the sidewalk. The roof was covered in colorful wafers. I'd bet anything my dad's 3D printer was responsible for that.

"Someone put a lot of effort into this," Jett said as we got out of the car.

I took Creepers's carrier from the back. He meowed in protest. He hadn't enjoyed the plane ride.

The yard had six-foot-tall gingerbread men with smiling faces.

"I feel like they're all looking at me," Boyd said. "It makes me shiver."

I fake gasped. "The mayor of Muddy Creek is scared of wooden gingerbread men?"

Boyd grinned. "Everyone's scared of something."

I had to admit, I wouldn't want to run into one of them in the dark. Their fixed candy smile and blank stare were the things of nightmares.

I turned and looked at Frank's house across the street. It had similar decorations. We'd seen at least six houses decorated as gingerbread houses when we drove into the neighborhood. I wondered what the winning house would get. I doubt it would be worth the money people must have put into the decorations.

"It's strange to wear short sleeves in December," Jett said. "It feels unnatural to go from snow to this in just a few hours."

"My skin doesn't even know what to do," I said. "It's like whiplash by weather."

"Ivy!" My mom burst out of the door and headed toward me with her arms open wide. Her light brown curls bounced as she ran.

I handed the carrier to Boyd, rushed toward her, and gave her a big hug. She smelled like cinnamon and everything good about Arizona. "I've missed you."

"Not as much as I've missed you! You have to visit more, or we're going to have to retire in Muddy Creek."

"I'm for that."

"I don't think I can give up the weather."

My parents would never move. They loved it here.

She looked over at Boyd. "Good to see you, Boyd. I was so excited you came. And Jett!" My mom hurried toward him, and I smiled as his eyes went wide. She wrapped him in a hug and gave him a loud kiss on the cheek.

He cleared his throat. "It's good to see you again, Candy." His face had taken on a reddish hue that I would have to tease him about later.

"I'm so excited for the wedding. I hope you two don't wait too long." My mom linked her arm with Boyd's and walked to the house.

Jett swallowed nervously, and I took his hand and rubbed it. "You're lucky she didn't get you on the lips," I whispered.

He smiled sheepishly and shook his head.

We entered the house, and a homesickness I hadn't realized I had settled in my stomach. Snowy landscapes had replaced the entryway paintings, and a wreath hung over the door. The stair railing in front of us was wrapped in pine with big red bows. My dad decorated the outside, but my mom took care of the inside.

I loved my memories of helping them as a kid. Wrapping the railing had been my job, and I'd taken pride in it.

I took the carrier from Boyd and set it on the floor. I opened it, and Creepers peeked out.

"Ivy!" my dad said, walking down the stairs. He grabbed me in a bear hug. Jett took a step back, probably worried my dad might give him the same treatment my mom had. My dad kept his arm over my shoulders and turned to shake Jett's hand. "Hello, Jett."

"Nice to see you, Mr. Clark," he said.

My dad held his hand out to Boyd. "Good to see you again."

"You have a great setup outside," Boyd complimented.

"Thanks. I'm planning on winning the competition."

I set my purse on a small decorative table. "What's the prize?"

"One thousand dollars."

"Wow. How much have you spent on everything?"

My mom rolled her eyes. "We aren't talking about that."

I laughed. "I see."

"Come into the kitchen. I have warm bread waiting for you." She scurried down the hall. My dad and Boyd followed.

Jett leaned close to me. "I forgot your dad's name."

"It's Hank."

"Right. I knew that. I'm a little nervous."

I kissed him quickly. "Don't worry. My parents are relaxed for the most part. Come on. Let's get some bread." I took his hand and dragged him to the kitchen.

"Come on, Creepers." He'd probably hide for a bit, but curiosity always won out.

Boyd and my dad were already sitting at the round oak table, and my mom was getting something from the fridge.

Two loaves of homemade bread sat cooling on the table. I sat down and motioned to the chair next to me. Jett sat, his back straight. He really was nervous.

"Here we go," my mom said, bringing two jars of jam to the table. She went back to the counter and grabbed a bread knife. "I was so excited when you all agreed to come. Last year was a sad year with only Hank and me." She handed the knife to my dad, and he began cutting the bread.

"When do they judge the houses?" Boyd asked.

My dad looked up. "Not until Christmas Eve. It's going to be a new thing in the area. Every Christmas, there will be a new theme."

My mom frowned. "That means new decorations every year. And you have to pay to participate in the competition. That's how they get the prize money."

Dad passed out slices of bread, and my mom gave everyone a small plate and a knife.

"Candy always made the best bread in Muddy Creek," Boyd said, spreading apricot jam on his piece.

"Aw, thanks, Boyd."

"I'm not just saying that," Boyd told Jett. "Candy won first place for her bread and jam more than once at the fair."

"And that was a long time ago," my dad said. "She improves it every year."

Boyd took a bite. "I think you're right."

I spread the plum jam on my bread. "What are the plans for the week?" Thinking we would be relaxing while visiting my parents would be wrong. My mom had too many Christmas traditions for the average person.

"We'll go downtown to see the lights, of course. Then we're hosting a get-together for the neighborhood. Fudge making is a must. We didn't make too many solid plans because we weren't sure what you all would be up for. I know I get crazy during the holidays."

"Remember the year we had the Christmas pig competition?" Boyd asked.

My mom laughed. "Oh yes. That was a bit out of control."

I ate my bread and listened to Boyd and my mom reminisce.

Jett finished his bread, and I stood and grabbed his hand. "I'm going to show Jett the tree." I led him into the living room. A large tree decorated with white lights and silver decorations stood tall in the corner. A bright star shone on top.

"That's a huge tree," Jett observed. I pulled him over to the white couch and had him sit, then I flipped on the fireplace. Flames jumped up. I smiled at the silver stockings hanging from the mantel. My mom had gotten stockings for Jett and Boyd.

I went to the couch and sat on Jett's lap. "Are you alright? You seem overwhelmed."

He wrapped his arms around me. "I'm not sure what my problem is. It's not like I haven't met your parents. I guess I've just never talked to your parents since we've been engaged. I'm not sure what to say to them."

I put my hand on his cheek and kissed him. "You aren't scared of criminals, but you're scared of my parents? Your face turned a nice shade of red when my mom kissed you."

He grinned. "I wasn't expecting that."

"Just relax."

"I'll be fine. I just need a minute to adjust. I'm not used to having time to think. It's weird not to have any responsibilities."

"But it's kinda nice, right?" I asked, running my fingers through his hair.

He smiled. "I think it will be." He leaned forward and pressed his lips to mine.

"We came all this way, and that's all you can think to do?" Boyd asked. "That's all you do back home."

My mom giggled.

Jett stood, almost dropping me to the floor. He caught me and helped me stand. Jett's face was pink again. I'd never seen him unnerved like this, and I thought it was adorable.

"What are we doing today?" I asked. It was already past noon, but my mom could pack a lot into a short amount of time.

"Well, someone's got to clean the entryway," my dad said. "We should have shown Ivy's cat where the litter box was."

I groaned. "Sorry."

"No worries," my mom said. "I bought a cheap litter box and put it in the mudroom. Food dishes too."

I hugged her. "You're the best."

"I know."

I found the mop and cleaned up Creepers's accident. He stood watching me. "You made a mess, buddy." He meowed and crawled around my legs. "Come on. I'll show you the litter box." I picked him up and carried him to the mudroom. I put him down, and he sniffed the floor.

I put the mop away, then went looking for the others. I found them out in the backyard. My dad was showing them his latest project, which appeared to be constructing a shed.

Creepers was at my heels. He doesn't usually go outside of his own free will, but he must be nervous about being in a new place. Boyd picked him up, and the cat relaxed against him.

"Where's your dog?" my mom asked Jett.

"José and Carrie agreed to take care of him."

She smiled. "I was so happy to hear those two got married."

"Hey, Hank!" a man called from over the fence.

My dad waved. "Hi, Wayne."

"Who do you have over there?"

My dad sighed. "My daughter's visiting from Kansas."

"I'll be right over."

"Great," he muttered. "Wayne can't handle anything going on without him knowing."

"How long has he lived here?"

"About a year. The Anderson's dog used to bug me, but I wish they would move back. Wayne Wright is more annoying than ten dogs."

"Shhh," my mom said. "He'll hear you."

The gate opened, and a man around my parents' age entered. He wore jeans and an untucked button-up shirt that was nearly popping from his well-padded stomach. He was bald on top, with bushy brown hair growing around the sides and the back.

"I'm Wayne Wright," he said, walking up to me. "I'm glad to finally meet you." He shook my hand. "I've been following you."

My eyes narrowed. "Following me?"

He adjusted his glasses. "Online. You've solved some interesting cases. Can I take a picture with you?" He pulled out his phone and put his arm around me. My mom gave me an apologetic smile as he took a picture.

"And who are these people?" he asked.

My mom gestured to Boyd. "This is Boyd Webster. He's an old friend, and this is Jett Malone. He's marrying Ivy."

"Ah! The sheriff and the mayor." He grabbed Jett's hand and pumped it up and down, then shook Boyd's. "I follow the Muddy Creek social media pages. You've been in some newspaper articles about Ivy as well. I'm a big fan of all of you. Can the three of you pose for a picture?"

I shared a look with Jett.

"Sure," Boyd said, grabbing my arm. The three of us stood together and smiled. I felt odd, but if we were co-operative, I hoped Wayne would leave soon.

"What do you think about Hank's decorations?" he asked.

"They look good," I said.

"Did you see mine? I'm not finished, but I'm getting there."

"I'll have to look." I'd only paid attention to Frank's since he and my dad were always competing.

"Have you called the news stations?" Wayne asked my dad.

"No, about what?"

Wayne rolled his eyes. "About your famous daughter being in town. I bet they'd do a story."

"Oh no," I protested. "I'm not famous, and I don't want to draw any attention. I just want a nice family holiday."

"Not famous? That's ridiculous. You have a lot of fol-lowers online."

I didn't know what to say. I wasn't sure how to respond. I kept things pretty low-key online.

"I started a website about you. It has information on all the cases you've helped solve."

"That's not uncomfortable," Boyd mumbled under his breath.

"It was good to see you, Wayne," my mom said. "We're going to have to let you go. We have some things planned."

He frowned. "Don't make yourselves too busy. Save me a dinner appointment before you leave."

My dad herded us into the house, and we sat in the front room.

"That was strange," Jett said, putting his arm over my shoulders.

"Sorry," my mom said. "We mentioned one time that you lived in Kansas, and Wayne kept asking questions. I think he's lonely. When he found out you solved a murder, he looked it up. He's been obsessed with you ever since."

"That's creepy," I said. "Can we avoid him?"

"Not easily. He invites himself to dinner about once a week."

"Let's not think about Wayne," my dad said. "Anyone else think it's time to make fudge?"

I nodded, grateful for the distraction and trying to shake off the weirdness of my conversation with Wayne.

Chapter 3

Creepers was going to be spoiled. My dad had always wanted a pet, but my mom never let us get one. Now he was following Creepers around, letting him do whatever he wanted. I'd seen him give the little beggar three cat treats in one day. And if I saw it three times, I was pretty sure he'd done it more.

"You're going to make him sick," I said. "Believe me, you don't want to clean cat puke out of the carpet."

"Fine, fine," my dad said. "That's the last one for today." Creepers rubbed up against his leg. "I think he wants more."

"Of course he does. That's why he has us—to stop him from overdoing it."

"I suppose." My dad sat on a stool at the kitchen island and grabbed a snowflake cookie from a platter. "So that Jett seems like a nice boy."

I smiled. "A nice boy? He's thirty-four."

"He's good to you?"

"Yep."

"I'm glad you found him. I hate the thought of you off in Kansas on your own."

"I'm definitely not on my own. I have Boyd and José, and lots of friends. It's been good for me."

"Your mom worries about you. She hates the thought of you looking into crimes."

"I'm careful."

That was mostly true. My mom would die if she knew some of the things I'd done. I only gave her the most minor details. She always worried about my fascination with mysteries.

A few situations I'd been in crossed my mind. Maybe I wasn't as careful as I claimed. It wasn't like I went looking for these things. It was more like they followed me.

The doorbell rang, and my dad got up. I followed him down the hallway. I was bored—my mom had taken Jett with her to the craft store to help carry things that were too heavy for my dad's back. Boyd had fallen asleep on the couch.

Dad opened the door. I couldn't see past him. He closed most of it, leaving just his head visible.

"What is it?"

"I'm from the news station," a man's voice said. "Can I talk to Ivy Clark?"

I cringed.

"No," Dad said. "She isn't interested in talking to you."

"We got a tip about her. We want to do a story about her life in Kansas."

My dad looked over his shoulder, and I shook my head. "She's not interested."

I turned and rushed up the stairs and down the hall to my old room. I went in and closed the door. My parents kept my room the same way it was when I moved out. I lay back on my twin bed and hoped no one else came by looking for me.

I rolled to my side and stared at my bookshelf. I should probably clean all my stuff out so my parents could use this room for something. Not that they needed it. My dad already had an office, and my mom had a craft room. They also had three guest rooms.

It was strange to be home again and not really feel at home. Muddy Creek had become the place where I belonged.

I lay there until I heard the door shut, then got up and looked out the window. A white Mini Cooper was pulling away from the house. Across the street, I could see Frank adding more lights to his tree. Frank had lived there as long as my parents had. He'd always reminded me of a TV host.

Perfectly combed white hair, a huge smile, and a voice that always sounded like he was announcing something.

Lillith Rodriguez, the neighbor next door to Frank, came outside and put her hands on her hips. She was frowning and saying something to him. I'd always avoided Lillith as a kid. If a ball went into her yard, no one dared to go get it if they knew she was home. She yelled first, then checked facts.

Her daughter, Chelsea, was my age, and it had always been awkward trying to come up with reasons not to go to her house.

Lillith reminded me of a cartoon villain. She was thin with sunken cheeks, and she always wore her hair in a tight braid. She was a principal, and I'd always been glad she never worked at my school.

Frank kept hanging lights, ignoring her. He worked for a marketing company. I didn't know what he did exactly, but he always seemed to have plenty of free time and money.

Lillith's arms swung around as she talked, then she stomped back across the lawn to her house. Frank kept working like she'd never been there. It seemed Frank had mastered the art of polite disregard.

My mom's car pulled into the driveway, so I went back downstairs. She opened the front door, and Jett carried in a big crate. My mom was always buying things like that and turning them into crafts. She could make the strangest thing into something amazing.

"Just put that over here," she said, pointing near a wall. Jett put it down and went back out for something else. "That's a tough guy you've got. You should move closer. He would be useful."

I grinned. "I'm not moving so you can boss Jett around."

"Boss?" She smiled. "Never. Suggest or beg, maybe."

Creepers ran past my feet. He was enjoying all the extra space.

The sun was starting to set, and I wanted to go to bed before my mom unveiled tomorrow's jam-packed itinerary. I wouldn't stand a chance against her holiday energy on less than eight hours of sleep.

When Jett finished helping my mom, we turned on a movie. If I went to bed as soon as it ended, I should get plenty of sleep. Boyd was still asleep on the couch.

"Boyd won't be able to sleep tonight," I observed.

"You'd be surprised," Jett said. "He sleeps more than anyone I've ever known."

"Ivy," my mom said, peeking into the room. "Wayne's here. He wants to talk to you."

I groaned. "Okay. You can start without me," I told Jett. "I've seen this movie a hundred times." I got up and went into my parents' front sitting room. Wayne sat in a chair, tapping his fingers on his leg.

He stood when he saw me. "Ivy. I hope it's okay I came. I was wondering if I could beg for your help."

"Don't stand for me," I said, coming in and sitting on the loveseat.

"I wanted to talk to you earlier, but there were too many people. I can pay you."

I narrowed my eyes. "For what?"

"I want you to figure out who is trying to kill me."

My eyes went wide. "What makes you think someone's trying to kill you?"

"All sorts of weird things have been happening. Things falling at my house and at work and almost hitting me. Cars whipping out of nowhere, trying to run me down. I've been lucky to get out of the way. I'm a big guy and not very agile. One of these days, my luck will run out."

"Have you talked to the police?"

"Yeah, but they think it's all in my head."

I wasn't sure what to think. I didn't know Wayne well enough to judge his sanity.

"Do you have enemies?"

"I think I annoy lots of people, but I wouldn't call them enemies."

"And you think someone is getting in your house to try to get you?"

His eyes opened as wide as they could go. He leaned forward. "Horrifying, isn't it?"

"Do you have cameras on your house?"

"No, never. I'm worried the government would use them against me. That's how it always starts. They watch you with your own equipment. I'm too smart for that."

I moved my mouth to the side and stared at him.

He slumped back. "Great. I can tell you think the same thing as the police. You'll all feel bad when I turn up dead."

"I'm not saying I don't believe you, but maybe you just have an overactive imagination?"

"Not at all. It's just started in the last month or so. When I found out you were here, I knew I had a chance. You have to help me."

I took a deep breath. "I don't know."

"If you don't, no one else will."

"Do you live alone?"

"Yep. Just me and my pet snake, Ginger."

"Has anyone else seen any of these things happen?"

"No. Whoever's after me doesn't want anyone to witness it."

"And you have no idea who it could be?"

"None at all. Well, some neighbors would love to see me disappear."

"Like who?"

"Frank Weller, for one."

Figures. Frank didn't even flinch when Lillith was yelling at him earlier. I doubted he'd flinch at a murder charge either.

Still, I didn't think Frank had it in him. "I think he's harmless. I've known him all my life."

"Then you know he wants to win the house decorating competition."

"He wouldn't kill you to win." I didn't add that Wayne's house was the most poorly decorated on the block. I could tell he was trying, but Christmas decorations weren't his talent.

"He might. He glares at me all the time now that I have my decorations up."

"Who else?"

"Lillith Rodriguez. She hates me."

"She hates most people."

"She thinks because she's a principal, she knows more than everyone else. She won't even consider theories about the moonwalk being fake. I understand that some people don't believe it, but she won't discuss it. She's allowing herself to be ignorant because she won't engage in normal conversation. I told her that, and it made her angry. She yelled at me in front of all the neighbors."

Yikes.

I didn't know what to say. I didn't want to offend Wayne, but I was with the police. He was imagining things or making them up.

"I would probably put your dad on the list, but I don't want to offend you. Hank seems like a decent guy, but I know he wants to win the competition."

I pushed a lock of blond hair from my eye. "My dad isn't trying to kill you."

"Maybe not, but someone is. Will you at least think about helping me?"

"Sure."

"I'll talk to you at your parents' party. Thanks. It's good to know someone might have my back."

I let him out and tried not to feel guilty. I passed Mom in the kitchen.

"What did Wayne want?" she asked.

"He thinks someone's trying to kill him, and he wants me to figure out who."

"That sounds like Wayne. I thought he just wanted to bring you a flat earther pamphlet. I have a drawer full."

"So you think he's making it up?"

She grabbed a rag from a drawer and got it wet. "I think he exaggerates, maybe to the point of believing the things he says. It's hard to know for sure."

"If I ignore it, I'll feel bad. Especially if something happens to him."

My mom wiped the table. "Last month, he told your dad about the time he saw Bigfoot. I would ignore it unless he asks again. I think it's all to get attention. I bet he doesn't even believe half the things he tells people."

"Do you need help?"

"Nope. I'm done here. Go cuddle with your sheriff."

No one had to tell me twice. I went into the living room and found Jett sound asleep. I looked from him to Boyd and frowned. It had been a busy day, but I'd hoped to stay up until the movie was over.

I sat next to Jett and snuggled up to him. He didn't move. I tried to watch the movie for a few minutes, but I was thinking about Wayne. He must be making it all up. If someone were breaking into his house and his office, someone would have seen. Probably. But maybe not. I'd broken into plenty of places and never been seen.

Jett yawned and pulled me close. "What did he want?"

"He thinks someone is trying to kill him, and he wants to pay me to figure out who."

He groaned. "Do we ever get a normal vacation?"

"I think he's imagining it or making it up."

"But it's going to bother you if you don't find out for sure."

I smiled. Jett knew me well. "Yes."

"You need to be careful."

"I don't think it's anything dangerous."

"But you need to remember that I have no jurisdiction here. If you get yourself into trouble, the police aren't going to look the other way."

"I don't think the police will be involved. I'll just look around his house and see if anything seems odd."

He nodded and pointed at the TV. "I'm not sure you should get to pick the movie."

I grinned. "Is that why you were asleep when I was only gone for five minutes?"

"Yep. This is rough."

"We don't have to watch it."

He leaned down and kissed me. "I wasn't planning on it."

Chapter 4

I leaned over and grabbed a package from the porch. The sun was just coming up, and everyone else was still asleep.

"Ivy!" Wayne said, scurrying across the lawn. "I was hoping to see you."

I placed the package on the floor behind me and stepped out. Christmas lights shone on all the nearby houses.

"Hi, Wayne."

"You have to come to my house to see what's happened. You'll have to believe someone's after me when you see this."

I took a deep breath and followed him across the lawn. His Christmas decorations were intense. He had more than anyone else, but they weren't well organized. He must have found a deal on blowup gingerbread men, because he had several. He wasn't keeping with the gingerbread house theme. There was a blowup dog that popped out of a present every few seconds, and a tree covered in cartoon ornaments. He'd blown something all over the grass that looked like snow.

I followed him into his house and wondered if I should have grabbed Jett or Boyd to come with me. There wasn't a single Christmas decoration inside. The door led straight into the living room. It was spotless. Brown leather furniture looked like it had never been touched, and a glass table almost sparkled.

"Come to the kitchen. This will prove to you someone's after me."

I followed him to the kitchen. I almost slipped on the tile floor. It was so clean.

"Careful," he said. "I wax it every other day."

"That's a lot if you're the only person who lives here."

"I've always felt the best way to keep an eye on your possessions is to keep them clean. Then, if anything is out of order, it's obvious. Don't you agree?"

"I suppose so." There was nothing on any surface that didn't have to be there. I couldn't even see a toaster. The black-and-white granite counters were spotless. A person would never look at his outdoor decorations and think the inside would look like this.

Wayne walked over to the fridge and threw it open. He pointed into the fridge. "See?"

I looked in and frowned. It looked like the inside of any fridge. Any clean fridge. "What am I looking at?"

His eyes narrowed. "You're the detective. Shouldn't you know?"

I held in an eye roll. "I'm not a detective."

"But you should be."

He might be right.

"I run a diner. Nothing in here looks weird to me."

"Sue's Diner," Wayne said. "I can't wait to eat there someday. I might go to Muddy Creek for my next vacation. You didn't bring José with you. I was hoping I could meet him."

I cringed. How much stuff could a person find online about us?

"I watched you all when you were in the online baking competition."

That made more sense. I looked over everything in the fridge, but for the life of me, I couldn't figure out what Wayne wanted me to see.

"Don't you see anything out of place?"

"I don't know your habits, so I'm not sure I could find anything wrong." I looked closer and wrinkled my nose. "Your mayo looks bad. You might want to chuck it."

He laughed. "Exactly! I knew you would see it."

"It's brown and probably moldy. Anyone would see that."

"Someone's trying to poison me. Look at the expiration date."

I picked up the jar and searched for the date. "It's expired by over a year."

He puffed out his chest. "Now, do you believe me?"

"I'm not sure expired mayo makes me think someone wants to kill you. I bet you just didn't notice it was old."

"Not likely. I clean out my fridge weekly. I might miss something that has expired once, but not week after week."

I blinked. "Trying to kill someone by putting expired food in their fridge doesn't make sense. Anyone who opened the mayo would see it was bad and toss it."

"I'm not saying the person after me is a criminal mastermind. I bet they're trying to be tricky. They want to catch me off guard with something small that people won't notice, and even if someone did, they would think I just ate bad food. Besides, that's not all. Come to my laundry room."

I followed him down a dark, narrow hallway and into a small room with a white washer and dryer. Above them was a cupboard. He pulled it open and grabbed a small bag of detergent. He handed it to me.

I studied the bag. There was a best-by date, but it wasn't for a few more months. Wayne watched me closely. I was going to have to make myself busy while I was here, so things like this didn't keep happening. I felt more sure than ever that no one was after Wayne.

"Open it," he said.

I unsealed it and glanced inside. It was half full of white and blue laundry powder. Since Wayne seemed to want me to find the problem, I shook it around to see if I found anything weird. A few clumps were the only thing I noticed, and I doubted even Wayne would think they were a problem.

I shook it around some more. An odor assaulted my nose, and I frowned and sniffed the detergent. It smelled... rotten. Maybe moldy?

An enormous smile slid across Wayne's face. "Aha! You got it! It smells bad."

"It must have gotten a little wet. That's why there are clumps inside."

"But how would it get wet? I didn't get it wet. That means someone tampered with it."

I rubbed my lips together. "I don't think someone would come into your house and get your laundry detergent wet. What's the point?"

"Mold can be toxic."

"If they killed you with something like that, they would be very lucky."

"Lucky?"

"I mean, lucky that they wanted it to kill you, and it did. It's improbable. You might have left the bag unsealed, and some moisture from the air got inside."

He adjusted his glasses, and his mouth turned down. "You think I'm crazy. Just like everyone else. Well, I have one more thing. Come on." He led me to his bedroom. It was as spotless as everything else. Against one wall was a big tank with a light on top.

"Is that your snake?" I asked.

"Yes. This is Ginger." He walked to the tank and opened a door on the top. He reached in and pulled out a small pink snake.

I ignored the chill that went over my arms and back. "It's pink."

"Yes, she's an albino corn snake. Pretty, isn't she?"

I nodded. "As far as snakes go." I knew most snakes weren't dangerous, but they still made me uneasy. The snake coiled around Wayne's arm, and I shivered.

"Ginger eats a pinky every week. Only one."

I raised my eyebrow. "A pinky?"

"A small mouse."

"Oh."

"Corn snakes aren't picky eaters. When you offer them food, they eat it. Last night was Ginger's feeding day, and guess what? She wouldn't eat it."

"Okay? I'm not sure what that means."

"It means someone else has been feeding her."

This was ridiculous. I was wasting time that I should have been spending with my family and friends.

"I'm not sure how someone feeding your snake would mean they were trying to kill you. I bet the snake wasn't hungry."

"How much do you know about snakes?" he asked, holding it out to me.

I took a step back. "Not much. What would the point of someone feeding the snake be?"

"They might be trying to scare me and make me uneasy. If I'm worried, I'm more likely to be killed by one of their subtle methods. I thought about going to my vacation house, but I don't run from my problems."

"I'm going to go," I said. "I need time to think."

"Great. Let me know if anything comes to you."

I nodded and hurried from his house. Jett stood on the sidewalk in front of my parents' house in a green button-up shirt and jeans, looking down the street. It was always strange to see him out of uniform.

"Morning," I said.

He spun around and took big strides over to me. "Where have you been?"

"At Wayne's. He had some evidence he wanted to show me."

Jett hugged me. "I was worried when I got up and couldn't find you."

"Sorry. I didn't plan on going. Wayne saw me picking up a package and told me he had proof someone was after him."

"You should have grabbed me."

"Probably."

"Did he have proof?"

"He had expired mayo, moldy laundry detergent, and a snake that won't eat. That's what he thinks is evidence."

Jett released me and frowned. "How is any of that evidence?"

"No clue. It was getting weird, so I told him I had to go think."

"If you ever go again, take me or Boyd with you."

I nodded. "I don't think he's a danger. Just odd."

He took my hand, and we walked back to the house.

"It's nice to have good weather," he said. "I could get used to warm Christmases."

"Last year was my first snowy Christmas. The snow makes it feel magical, but I would prefer having it only on Christmas."

We went into the kitchen and sat at the table.

He grinned slyly. "If it only snowed on Christmas, we never would have been snowed in that time at the Clements, and you never would have been able to trick me into kissing you under the mistletoe."

"That's a story I want to hear," my mom said, entering the room.

I glared playfully at Jett, ignoring his embarrassed look. "That's not what happened."

My mom sat at the table. "What did happen?"

"The Clements hung mistletoe over their kitchen island," I said. "Who does that? I didn't see it, and I was mixing something standing under it."

"And Jett found you there?"

"Yes, after Boyd or José pointed it out."

"Best day of my life," Jett said. "I'd been waiting for something like that to happen for months."

I couldn't believe he admitted that in front of my mom.

Boyd came in, still wearing his bathrobe. He grinned. "I remember that." He sat next to my mom. "Ivy was so flustered she went and stared into an empty freezer for five minutes."

I scowled. "It wasn't empty. It was full of ice."

They all laughed.

"So was that your first kiss?" my mom prodded.

I nodded and tried to think of a way to change the subject.

She tapped her lip. "Why don't we have any mistletoe? I should get some."

"Those two only needed it once," Boyd said.

I glared at him. "What do you know, Boyd?"

He laughed. "I catch the two of you in a lip-lock all the time."

Jett leaned his elbows on the table. "You wouldn't if you knew how to knock."

"Who wants oatmeal?" my dad asked, coming up behind me.

My mom tilted her head. "Don't be silly, Hank. You don't go on vacation to eat oatmeal. Let's go out for some pancakes. Let me go brush my hair." She stood and hurried from the room.

My dad winked. "Mention oatmeal around Candy, and you always get to go out to eat."

I smiled. "I always wondered why you suggested oatmeal so much, but we rarely ate it."

Boyd stood and stretched. "If we're going out, I better shower. I'll be back down in a few."

"I'm going to check on Creepers before we go." I went up to my room. Creepers was in the same place I'd left him. Curled up on my bed. I believed the saying *Let sleeping dogs lie* applied to cats as well. Creepers hated being woken.

Wayne's house had been silent. This one was filled with laughter and sarcasm—the way it should be. I couldn't help feeling bad for Wayne. He must get lonely.

My phone rang, and I pulled it from my pocket. It was José.

"Hello?"

"Hi, Ivy."

"How's the diner?"

"It's great. I made a new cream pie that went over well yesterday."

"Nice. You'll have to make it again when we get home."

"I will. I just called to tell you I hired two more servers and another cook."

"Really? That's great news."

"Yep. If this keeps up, everyone will be able to work normal schedules."

I'd been hoping for something like this. "Has it been busy?"

"No. We got more snow. That's keeping most people away. It makes it easier to train people when things are calm. It's giving Anton and Livy too much free time. I keep finding them holed up on the stairs."

"Hey!" I heard Anton say in the background.

I smiled.

"I didn't tell her what you're doing on the stairs," José told him. "Anyway, things are going well. You don't need to worry. Are you all relaxing?"

"Something like that. The guy next door has some weird obsession with me. He thinks someone's trying to kill him, and he wants me to figure out who. He follows all our social media in Muddy Creek."

"You just can't catch a break. Be careful."

"I don't think anyone's after him. He's a little eccentric. Hey, my family is having a fudge-making competition later today. I'm not a huge fan of fudge. Do you have any tips for me?"

"I have a good recipe. I'll email you."

"Thanks, José. You're the best."

"True. Enjoy the rest of your vacation."

"Thanks."

I hung up and went to a search engine to see what it meant when snakes wouldn't eat. I had to have something to tell Wayne the next time he talked to me. There were several reasons. Snakes might not eat when they were shedding. Wayne's snake was small, so she might be ready to shed. I didn't know how big corn snakes got, but it had to be bigger than she was. It could also have been from stress or environmental factors.

I could believe any of those things. They all made more sense than someone sneaking in to feed her. I couldn't see any reason for a person to do that.

The next time I saw Wayne, I could give him some suggestions. Whether he would listen or not was anyone's guess.

Chapter 5

"This doesn't resemble fudge in any way," Jett said, looking into his nine-by-nine pan. He picked up his rubber spatula and tried to spread it around some more. I peeked around him. His fudge had the consistency of dirt mixed with marshmallow.

"We won't judge you," I said, then I smiled. "Actually, we will. It's a competition, after all."

He grinned at me. "But you like me for my other skills, right?"

"What other skills?" Boyd asked. "Arresting people?"

"That's one."

"He has more," I said, trying not to look too proud of my own fudge. I'd used cookies-and-cream candy bars and walnuts. José sent me the recipe.

"We don't want to hear about his kissing skills," Boyd teased.

"Good," I said, "because I wasn't going to tell you about them."

"I do have them, though," Jett said, rubbing the spatula across the fudge.

My parents had gone out to get some things for their neighborhood party, and they would judge the fudge this evening. If I didn't win, I would call out my parents. Boyd's fudge smelled burnt and had an odd darkish color.

"Right, Ivs?" Jett asked.

"Hmm?" I'd stopped listening.

Boyd laughed. "I guess that means your skills are mediocre."

"You're killing me, Ivs."

"You two are ridiculous." I put my pan on the table and kissed Jett's jaw. "Don't let Boyd rile you. He's just jealous he doesn't have anyone to kiss."

"Ha ha," Boyd said. "I'll have you know I'm quite popular among the over-sixty crowd in Muddy Creek."

I laughed. "You are. No one can deny that."

"So what do we do with the fudge?" Boyd asked.

"Put it in the fridge. Then we don't tell who made each one so it's a fair vote."

"Why wouldn't it be fair?" Jett wondered.

"Because they might vote for one of you to be polite."

"And you think they won't know who made the only one that looks good? It won't be hard to guess. Everyone will know the owner of the diner made it."

I smiled. "We still don't know what they taste like. Taste trumps looks every time."

"I'm sure the best-looking one will also be the best-tasting one."

"That's not always how it works," I protested even though I was sure mine would be the best.

Jett pushed his fudge aside and smiled at me. "But sometimes it is." He came over and put his hands on my waist. "Do you want to test it?"

"Gag," Boyd said. "You two were cute at first, but now you need to give it a break. Ivy needs a mystery to solve or something."

Jett dropped his hands and sat on a kitchen chair. "Next time we go on vacation, I vote we leave Boyd at home."

Boyd chuckled. "Hurry and get married, and you can go somewhere all by yourselves and be as cringy as you want."

"Where do you want to go on our honeymoon?" Jett asked me.

I shrugged. "I haven't thought about it."

A pounding on the door made it so I didn't have to decide. I went to the door and pulled it open to see Wayne.

"Hi, Wayne."

"Something else has happened," he said. "Hurry and come."

I frowned. "Let me find my shoes and I'll be over."

"Come to the backyard."

I nodded and closed the door. I grabbed my shoes, sat on the floor, and pulled them on.

"Who was it?" Jett asked, coming down the entryway.

"Wayne. He wants me to go see something in his backyard."

"I'm coming."

I held out my hands, and he pulled me to my feet. "Sounds good."

We walked over to Wayne's fence and went through. He was standing, looking at the ground.

"Hey, Wayne," I said.

"Come here," he commanded. "Look at this."

We went to where he was pointing. The grass was soaked, and footprints were visible on the wet spots.

"Someone got this spot wet, then walked on it and made it a bit muddy. What do you have to say now?"

I shared a look with Jett.

"I'm not sure."

"Someone's been in my yard, and they were messing with things."

Jett raked a hand through his brown hair and looked around. "Nothing seems to be ruined."

"No, but someone wants to scare me. It's a warning."

"It's a bit subtle for a warning."

Wayne's eyes fixed on him. "Of course. They can't be obvious. Whoever it is wants it to look like nothing's going on. They do small things that they know no one but me will pay attention to."

"This could be from a leaky sprinkler."

"What about the footprints?"

Jett looked at Wayne's muddy boots. "It looks like you walked on it."

"You're a sheriff. Can't you do a more thorough search?"

"I'm off duty, and even if I wasn't, I have no authority in Arizona."

"What do you have to say?" he asked me.

I pressed my lips together and shook my head. Wayne dragging me over to show me pretty much nothing was getting a bit old.

He sighed. "I see. So much for getting the help of the mighty Ivy Clark."

Jett turned to the side and smiled.

"We're having fudge tonight if you want to come," I said.

Wayne nodded. "I'll be there."

We left him standing there. I felt guilty, but I wasn't sure what he wanted me to do. His explanation didn't make sense to me, so I didn't know how to help him.

"That guy needs some friends," Jett said as we walked across my parents' yard.

"Do you think that's the problem?"

"It's hard to say, but he definitely seems to be looking for attention. It might be good to ask around about him. Make sure he isn't a danger to anyone."

"He doesn't seem to be."

He rubbed his chin. "No, but what else might he do for attention?"

"It might be something else. Maybe he really thinks someone is doing it."

"It's hard to tell."

"Back to the fudge?"

He grinned. "I'm pretty sure there's nothing else I can do to make mine edible. I'm excited to try yours, though."

"Wait!" Wayne called, jogging toward us.

We stopped and waited for him to catch up.

"I'll just come with you now and wait until the fudge is ready."

I tried not to cringe. "It could take a while."

"That's alright. I spend a lot of time with Hank and Candy. They won't mind." He began walking to the front door. I looked at Jett, and he shrugged.

Wayne walked into the front door without an invitation. He was just a neighbor, but he acted like part of the family. Like he'd earned a seat we hadn't offered. We went in after him and followed him to the kitchen. Boyd was closing the fridge.

Wayne sat at the table. "What's it like to be mayor of Muddy Creek?"

Boyd turned. "Well, it isn't boring."

"You only got voted in because your opponent was killed, is that right?"

"Yep."

He knew a lot for someone who didn't live in Muddy Creek.

"He would have won anyway," I said. "People liked him more than the former mayor."

"I want to hear all about it. Reading things is great, but hearing it from people who have experienced it is more exciting."

Boyd sat at the table. "What do you want to know? I have plenty of time."

I grabbed Jett's arm and pulled him from the room. "I don't want to listen to this. Boyd might talk for hours. Do you want to play a game?"

"So long as it isn't Boogle."

I smiled. "You're such a poor loser."

"I still don't think Yclept is a word."

"It's in the dictionary."

"I bet they put it in there to annoy people."

"I would have beat you, even without using it."

"Probably."

"There's no probably."

"Let's play Risk."

My mouth turned down. "I don't believe in doing math when I'm playing a game."

He grinned. "Or you know I'll beat you."

"You were brutal last time, and it took hours. Aren't there any games we're more even at?"

"Not that we've played so far. We need a new one."

"We could do a puzzle."

Jett made a fake snoring sound.

"We could go get ice cream."

"That sounds better. Ice cream in December is a foreign idea to me. Let's do it."

"Your cookies smell amazing," my mom said as she whisked something in a pan. "Our guests will be spoiled."

"It's too bad that it's hard to keep them warm. They taste so much better," I said.

"They're good room temperature as well."

"But by tomorrow, they'll be a day old. They won't be as good when they aren't fresh. It's fine, though. No one will care anyway when you bring out your famous eggnog."

"We should have saved the fudge for the party."

I grinned. "I'm not sure that would be neighborly."

My mom laughed. "Yours tasted great. I'll admit the other two could use work."

"I don't love Jett for his cooking skills. I'm sorry I invited Wayne to the fudge contest. I didn't realize he would stay so long."

"We've come to accept that Wayne is going to show up whenever we do anything. We figure it's better to expect him than to get annoyed. He's not that bad once you realize you need to take him with a grain of salt."

"Do you hear something?" I asked, straining my ears.

My mom was quiet for a minute. "Is someone yelling?"

"I'll go look."

I walked through the house and peeked out a front window. Frank and Wayne were standing in the street, and Frank was shouting. I'd seen Frank get competitive before, but I'd never heard him yell. I opened the window a crack so I could hear.

"Stay out of my yard!" Frank yelled.

"I didn't do anything!" Wayne said. "I just came over to borrow something."

"That's a lie. You ruined some of my decorations! You are much too competitive."

"I would never."

"I was out here ten minutes ago, and everything was fine. Now I come out, and things are broken, and you're standing there with a piece of one of my decorations."

"I saw it was broken, and I was going to take it to you."

Wayne always had an excuse. But he was the one holding the evidence.

Frank muttered something I couldn't hear.

Lillith came stomping toward them, her black braid as tight and neat as ever. "What are you two yelling about?" she asked, almost as loud as they were.

"This is none of your business!" Frank shouted.

My eyes went wide. I'd never seen Frank like this. He must be really mad about his decorations.

"It's my business when you're interrupting the entire neighborhood!"

"This is why everyone avoids you!"

Lillith's mouth fell open in shock. It only lasted a moment. Her eyes narrowed, and her jaw was set. She pulled back her arm and punched Frank in the shoulder. I bet she was aiming for his face, but she's short, and Frank is over six feet. He grabbed her arm and twisted it behind her back.

He marched her over to her house and pushed her onto her lawn. It might be time to call the police. I grabbed my phone and watched Lillith pop up and charge at Frank. Wayne took the opportunity to hurry to his house. I frowned at the screwdriver poking out of his pocket. Lillith grabbed Frank around the waist, and they both dropped to the ground. She sat on him and slapped him repeatedly.

Right as I was about to dial, Jett pulled up in the rental car. He jumped out and ran over, pulling Lillith off Frank.

"Stay away from me, you psycho!" Frank said, pointing at Lillith. She struggled against Jett, who had her held tightly against him, her arms pinned to her sides. "I don't know why I put up with you for so long!"

Jett said something to Frank. I couldn't hear since he wasn't yelling. Frank took a deep breath, then stomped to his house. Jett said something to Lillith. She nodded, and he released her. She ran to her house, and the door slammed shut behind her. Jett shook his head and came to the house. I hurried and met him at the door.

"What did you say to them?" I asked.

"What?"

"I was looking out the window. I was about to call the cops."

"What was going on?"

I told him what I heard.

"Hmm. I told the guy to get in the house, and thankfully, he did. I told the woman I'd let her go if she calmed down. I half expected her to kick me in the shins before she left. Are they all coming to your parents' party?"

"Probably."

"I hope they calm down before tomorrow."

"Frank's usually calm. Even when he's being a jerk, he usually acts mellow. When he and my dad tease each other, it's all in fun."

"I think Wayne rubs people the wrong way."

"I could see that. Lillith is always on fire about something. I'm surprised she's never attacked anyone before. I've always been scared of her."

"Well, we better make sure they all stay away from each other tomorrow, or we might have a repeat."

Chapter 6

The main floor of my parents' house was packed with neighbors. Nothing about these get-togethers my parents threw was organized. The reason people came was to eat great food and socialize. I might start something like this at the diner. Everyone on the street was invited, and most people came. It was more socializing than I liked to do at one time, but my mom thrived in these situations.

"Ivy!" a woman said from behind me. I turned to see Chelsea Rodriguez, Lillith's daughter. She wore a tight red dress that almost reached her knees and red heels. I suddenly wished I wasn't wearing jeans and a sweater. At least I'd curled my hair.

I pasted on a fake smile. "Chelsea. Good to see you. It's been a while." Chelsea had been my friend in elementary school, but we'd grown apart as we got older. Chelsea became a member of the drill team in high school, and that had been the end of it. She'd become superficial, and she ditched me. We were still polite when we ran into each other, but we both annoyed each other without admitting it.

"I've heard a lot about you lately," she said. "You moved to Nebraska to be a server?"

"No, I moved to Kansas. I own a diner there."

"Oh. How... quaint."

"What are you doing these days?" I asked even though I wanted to end the conversation.

"Busy, busy. That's my life. I teach yoga, and I volunteer at my mom's elementary school once a week. I hardly have time to breathe."

"I've always wanted to do yoga, but I never have."

"Didn't you teach aerobics before you left?"

I nodded. "For a while. Now I only teach Zumba."

Chelsea rolled her eyes. "Zumba is such an odd fad. You'd better keep up on your aerobics. I'm fairly certain Zumba will be gone in a few years."

I ground my teeth together. "I don't need to teach it. I just do it for fun. I've had a lot of interest." I wouldn't tell her my entire class was made up of people old enough to be my grandma. That wouldn't impress her. I preferred people that age, but Chelsea had always been into the latest trends.

"That's nice. I should give you my hairstylist's name. I just found her last year, and she is so talented." Chelsea pushed her silky brown hair over her shoulder. "She might be able to get you in while you're in town. She can touch up those roots for you."

This was how every conversation with Chelsea went. I always regretted the way I started trying to outdo her. I wasn't normally that competitive, but Chelsea brought it out in me.

"My schedule is too full, but thanks," I said.

"My mom said a news van was here the other day. What was that about?"

I hadn't seen a news van. Only the person in the car who had come by. My dad must have sent them away like he did the first guy.

"I've solved a few mysteries," I said. "They wanted to talk to me about it." I wouldn't have said that to anyone but Chelsea because I was usually embarrassed by the attention.

Her eyes narrowed. "What kind of mysteries?"

"Murders."

She laughed. "I thought you were serious for a minute."

"I am. You can ask Wayne. He'll tell you all about it."

"Gross. I'm not talking to him." She rubbed one of her long silver hoop earrings between her fingers. "Someone needs to get him out of this neighborhood. He drives everyone crazy. He made my mom and Frank get into a big fight yesterday."

"Yeah, I saw that."

"I'm glad we can catch up. You know what? I know this guy who I should totally set you up with. Are you free tomorrow night? His name's Steve German."

My eyebrow rose. "I know Steve." Steve was one of the most boring guys I'd ever known. He was scared of girls to a crazy extent. At least he had been in high school. "I have a boyfriend. In fact—"

"Oh, don't give me that. If you had a boyfriend, your parents would have mentioned it when they talked to my mom."

"Why would I lie about that?"

"The same reason anyone lies about anything. To make themselves look good."

I was going to crack my teeth before this conversation was over. "Maybe that's the way you do things."

She waved her hand through the air. "That's how everyone does things."

"Hey." Jett came up behind me and put his hand on my back. Perfect timing. I know I shouldn't use Jett to make someone jealous, but Chelsea wasn't just someone, and Jett could make any woman drool.

I smiled up at him. "Jett, this is my old friend, Chelsea. Chelsea, this is my fiancé, Jett."

Chelsea's eyes almost popped out of her head as he offered his hand.

"Nice to meet you," he said.

She gave a small giggle. "Nice to meet you. Where are you from, Jett?"

"Kansas."

"Wow. I didn't know Kansas had guys like you."

Jett's brows came together, and he looked at me in confusion. I just smiled.

"Do you want to go out back for a few minutes?" he asked me. "It's getting stuffy in here."

"Sure. It was nice to see you, Chelsea." I linked my arm with Jett's and let him lead me out to the backyard. Several people were chatting in small groups out back. Christmas music played on my dad's big speakers.

"What's going on?" he asked. "You looked about ready to knock your friend out. I know that look."

My mouth turned down. "I know. I struggle with Chelsea. She ditched me in high school, and now whenever we talk, I feel like we're trying to be politely rude to each other. I don't know why I let her get on my nerves. I always walk away feeling like a loser after I talk to her."

"You're never a loser."

"Yeah, well, I feel like I won this time."

"Oh?"

I grinned. "I have you."

He rolled his eyes. "That's not impressive."

"You obviously weren't watching Chelsea."

"Why would I? I have you."

My heart melted as he wrapped his arms around me. I rested my head on his chest and sighed. "I know I shouldn't be petty around her, but she brings it out in me. She's always trying to show me up, and I let her get me riled up."

"You don't need to compare yourself to anyone. I think you're perfect."

I grinned slyly and looked up at him. "Even when I'm messing up your cases?"

He chuckled. "Okay, maybe not then."

"I'm embarrassed I act the way I do around her. I almost ran upstairs and changed into my black dress."

He kissed my nose. "I'll admit, I like that dress, but I like you no matter what you're wearing."

"Hey, everyone!" Wayne called out. He stood on the porch holding a goblet of eggnog. He held it in the air and swayed slightly to the side. "Merry almost Christmas!" He stumbled down the stairs and began talking to the person nearest him.

I tilted my head as I watched him. "My mom doesn't put alcohol in her eggnog. Why's he acting drunk?"

Jett shrugged. "Attention, maybe? We should probably keep an eye on him."

Frank and Lillith stood near a tree, talking. None of the hostility from yesterday hung around them. Lillith was even smiling.

"That's odd," Jett said. "I would think they would avoid each other after yesterday."

"They have an interesting relationship," Wayne said from behind us.

I jumped and spun around.

Wayne finished off his eggnog. "The two of them are on and off."

I studied them. "You don't mean... dating?"

"I do."

"I grew up across the street from them, and they never seemed to like each other."

"From what I understand, they've been involved in some way or another for over two decades."

"Who told you?" I couldn't believe I would miss something like that.

"Frank."

"Strange."

"It's not a healthy relationship," he said. "I'm going to get some more eggnog." He stumbled away.

"Is he drunk?" I asked. "If so, he must have been before he came."

"I think he's faking. He must think the eggnog has alcohol."

"That's so strange. Not as weird as Lillith and Frank being a couple. I always thought they hated each other."

"People are peculiar. Do you want to dance?"

I looked around at all the people. No one was dancing. "Dance to Christmas music?"

"Why not?"

Chelsea walked out onto the porch.

"Sure." I put my arms behind his neck, and we swayed slowly to the music. I needed to get over my Chelsea issues, not make them worse, but I enjoyed the loathing look she sent my way.

A minute later, Wayne came stumbling back out with more eggnog. He bumped into someone, but thankfully didn't spill on them. The man ignored him and stepped away.

Chelsea walked over to us. "Someone needs to make Wayne leave. He's going to cause a scene."

We stopped dancing, and I turned to her. "If you don't want him here, you can talk to my dad."

"Can't you get rid of him?"

"He hasn't done anything too bad."

"So you want to wait until he does?"

"I'll keep an eye on him," Jett said.

Chelsea shrugged. "I guess it doesn't hurt me. It's not my party. You know he's up to something. I saw him walking down the street two nights ago, with a shovel and a headlamp. You can't tell me that's innocent."

My eyes narrowed. "That is odd. I wonder what he was doing."

Chelsea shrugged. "Digging for treasure, burying bodies? With Wayne, who knows?"

She smiled at Jett and walked away.

"She reminds me of my cousin Tania," I said.

"I can see it. How is Tania doing?"

I wrinkled my nose. "You really think we stayed in contact?"

He shrugged. "I figured you might still hear what's happening with her."

"I'm not sure whether my mom is keeping tabs on her or not. She hasn't said anything, and I don't want to ask. I doubt she wants to talk to me."

"Should we go back in?"

I nodded. We went to the house and found the living room full of people listening to Boyd tell a story. I smiled as I listened. I would guess the story was about five percent true. I'd learned something in the time I'd met Boyd. If he had an audience, he had a story. He sat on a chair with Creepers on his lap.

I left Jett to listen to the story and went to see if my mom needed help. She was in the kitchen talking to someone I didn't know.

"Where's my drink?" Wayne asked, coming in. "I just had it."

Frank followed him. "It's right here. You left it on the ground outside."

Wayne yanked it from Frank's hand, slopping it on his wrist. Frank frowned and grabbed a napkin from the table. Wayne held up the goblet and grinned. "That's some powerful stuff you make, Candy."

Frank rolled his eyes. "Candy doesn't put alcohol in her eggnog."

"Nope, I don't," my mom agreed.

Wayne looked into his goblet. "Hmm. Someone must have spiked mine."

Everyone ignored him and went back to what they were doing.

My eyes narrowed. It sounded like Wayne had been at the house enough that he should know my mom's eggnog would be alcohol free. So who exactly was he pretending for? I thought about Chelsea talking about the shovel. I wondered if Wayne was ruining people's decorations.

I jumped when the sound of shattering glass hit my ears. Wayne had dropped his goblet. Eggnog covered the floor and his pant leg. He stared forward, his face pale.

"Are you alright?" I asked him.

My mom began picking up pieces of glass.

I squinted as I studied him. "Wayne?"

"I need to go home," he muttered.

"I'm not sure that's a good idea."

He shook his head as if clearing out a fog. "I'm fine." He smiled. "Sorry about the mess. I need to go to bed. Come over tomorrow at noon," he said, smiling too widely. "You can watch me feed Ginger." The way he said it felt... final. Like he was wrapping up a performance.

Watching a snake eat a mouse was not on my list of priorities.

"I'll walk you home," my dad said, taking Wayne's arm. Once they left the kitchen, normal conversation resumed.

"Wayne is the only person I know who can get drunk off eggs and vanilla," Frank said. A few people laughed, and Lillith pushed her way over to Frank.

"There should be ways to keep people like Wayne out of our neighborhood," she said. "A vote or something."

I watched a few people exchange looks. No one said anything, but I couldn't shake the feeling that Lillith wasn't the only one who'd fantasized about giving Wayne the boot.

Were they thinking the same thing I was—that if enough neighbors got annoyed, Wayne might be quietly pushed out? Not a formal vote, but the kind where people stopped inviting you to things, stopped answering your calls, and hoped you got the hint.

It was a strange thing to feel sorry for him, especially when he kept acting so weird. But part of me wondered what all this attention-seeking would turn into if the whole street turned their backs on him.

Lillith probably shouldn't talk about voting people out of the neighborhood. She wasn't at the top of people's list of favorites. I know I'd always been scared of her.

My mom looked at me and winked. "I think it's time to bring out Ivy's cookies."

Chapter 7

I curled a few pieces of hair that I hadn't pinned on my head and let them fall around my face. I was glad I hadn't caved and worn my dress yesterday. Today, we had lunch at a fancy restaurant, and this was the only dressy thing I brought.

Once I was happy with my hair, I grabbed my strappy black shoes and pulled them on. It had been a while since I'd dressed up. I always felt self-conscious when people were looking at me.

"What do you think?" I asked Creepers. He stared blankly at me, then yawned. "That bad, huh?" He jumped into the bathtub and curled up. "That's a horrible place for a nap." He ignored me and closed his eyes.

My parents had made reservations at this restaurant months ago. They must have had high hopes that I would come. Or maybe they'd meant to take friends, and it fell through.

"Ivy? You coming?" my dad called.

I walked into the hall and over to the stairs, then took a deep breath. Everyone would comment, and I was going to feel ridiculous. That was one problem with dressing up a few times a year. Everyone was surprised and thought they had to compliment me. I walked down the stairs and tried to pretend I was wearing jeans and a T-shirt.

Boyd whistled. I felt the temperature in my face rise.

"Oh stop," I said. I glanced at Jett, and my stomach flopped. He was wearing a suit, and he made it look good. His eyes were shining, and he smiled at me.

"You look nice," my mom said.

"Nice?" Jett lifted his eyebrows. "You look—"

I grabbed his arm and pulled him toward the door. "Let's go."

He laughed, and we walked to the rental car. We were going to meet my parents and Boyd at the restaurant. "You need to learn to take compliments."

I looked over at Wayne's house and ignored him. "I wonder if we should check on Wayne."

He opened the car door for me. "Now you're changing the subject."

I tilted my head. "What do you want me to talk about?"

"Compliments."

"You look amazing."

He rolled his eyes. "Not complimenting me."

I put my arms around him. "But it's true."

"And you look beautiful."

"Thank you," I muttered before he kissed me.

We got into the car and drove down the street. I still felt like someone should check on Wayne. He hadn't looked great last night, and who would check on him besides us?

All through lunch, I found my mind going back to Wayne. I jiggled my leg and ignored the conversation around me. The restaurant was nice, but the food wasn't any better than at any other places I'd been.

Jett leaned toward me and whispered, "What's going on?"

"I'm worried about Wayne."

"What about Wayne?" my dad asked.

"He didn't look well yesterday. Do you think he's okay?"

"I'm sure he is."

"He wasn't making a lot of sense. He said that Frank and Lillith have been dating for years. I figure he must be mistaken. I can't imagine them together."

My parents looked at each other.

"Where have you been?" my mom teased. "Those two have been a source of neighborhood gossip for years."

"How did I miss that?"

"I think you were always scared around Lillith, so you didn't notice."

"Chelsea never said anything."

My mom shrugged. "They aren't the best couple. They were engaged once, but they had a huge fight and called it off."

"It can't be a healthy relationship. She was smacking him in the face the other day, and then they were all happy together last night."

"I've given up on trying to figure those two out."

The rest of lunch passed smoothly, and the moment we pulled up to the house, I convinced Jett to go to Wayne's house.

I knocked on the door, and we waited. When no one came, Jett pounded harder. Nothing. I bit my lip. "Someone needs to go in and see if he's there."

"You can't break into someone's house for no reason."

"I have a reason."

"Do your parents have his number?"

"Probably." I grabbed his hand and pulled him across the yard. Something in me was sure there was a problem. I dragged him into the house and into the kitchen. My mom, dad, and Boyd were sitting at the table talking.

"Do you have Wayne's number?" Jett asked.

"Yep," my dad said. "Why do you want it?"

I tapped my toe on the floor. "He isn't answering the door."

My dad pulled out his phone and scrolled, then gave me the number. I plugged it into my phone and listened to it ring. It went to voicemail.

"Hey, Wayne. It's Ivy. Give me a call if you get this."
I hung up and looked at Jett. "We need to bust into his
house."

"That's skipping a few steps. Call the police and ask for
a welfare check. They can go in and make sure everything's
okay."

I nodded and called the police. When I explained to the
person on the phone why I was calling, they sighed.

"If he was seen last night, he's probably just out for the
day," the woman said. "Besides, Wayne Wright is flagged
for making unnecessary calls. He wastes police time and
resources."

"But he isn't the one calling. I'm a concerned neighbor."

"Nothing you said sounds like a reason to pry. If you
don't see him in two days, feel free to call back." The line
went dead.

"In two days, anything could happen."

"Why are you suddenly a Wayne supporter?" Boyd
asked.

"I'm not. I'd just feel bad if he passed out and hurt
himself or something. Besides, he invited me to watch him
feed his snake. He should be home."

"He was acting weird last night. He probably doesn't
remember saying that," Jett said.

I shook my head. "I'm going to check inside his house."

Jett took my shoulders. "Ivs, you're going to get in trouble. You can't break into someone's house just because

they don't answer the door or the phone. What if he's feeling sick and doesn't want to deal with people?"

I frowned. "What if he fell and hit his head and he's bleeding to death?"

My mom let out a slow sigh. "You've always seen a mystery in everything."

"I can't let you go alone, and I can't go with you," Jett said. "If I get caught, I could lose my job. I would get in more trouble than a normal person."

"You don't have to come."

"I'll come," Boyd said.

"This is crazy," my mom muttered. "Just stay in and we'll watch a Christmas movie."

"Nope. Come on, Boyd."

Boyd followed me out the door, and Jett trailed us.

"Ivs, come on. Just knock again, then wait a few hours," he said. We walked to the door, and Jett pounded on it. Nothing.

"His curtains are open," Boyd said. "If we find a ladder, we can look inside."

I walked to the window he pointed out. It was too high to see in, but only barely. "Lift me up a little," I told Jett.

With a sigh, he grabbed me around the upper legs and lifted me. I held the window frame and pressed my face against the glass.

"This isn't the best outfit for this," Jett muttered.

I ignored him. "I don't see anything. Let's go around back." He put me down, and I was careful not to twist my ankle in my heels. We went around the house, and I knocked on the door. He didn't answer. I twisted the knob, and it opened.

"Ivy..." Jett warned.

Boyd chuckled. "Jett's the kid who tags along, worrying about getting in trouble. Things have changed since high school."

Jett grinned slightly. "What do you know about me in high school?"

"Enough to know there were a lot of shocked people when you went to the academy."

"I wasn't that bad."

"But you weren't an angel either."

"Man. People never let you live down a few high school pranks."

I looked into the dark kitchen. "Wayne?" I called, then stepped into the house. Boyd was right behind me. "Are you coming?" I asked Jett.

"Nope. I'm going back and watching a Christmas movie with your parents."

"Good idea." I shut the door and flipped on the light. I pulled out gloves and put them on.

"He's probably going to stand out there until we come out."

I smiled. "Probably. I get where he's coming from. I'm sure I make things hard on him.

He can't go against the rules of his job, and I'm always doing something I probably shouldn't."

We walked into Wayne's bedroom. His bed was messy. That didn't seem right. I checked Ginger's cage. I could only see a small part of the pink snake. She was burrowed in her coconut shavings.

I wandered around, but when I didn't see anything, I went to the next room. I hadn't seen it the last time I came. It was an office. My eyes went wide when they landed on a spot on the floor that looked suspiciously like a one-foot trail of blood.

"What does that look like?" I asked.

"Looks like someone was bleeding and possibly dragged," Boyd said.

I swallowed. "Dragged where? I saw nothing in the hall." I opened the closet and looked all around the office.

A chair was tipped over, and one of its legs was broken. The desk drawers were open and appeared to have been rifled through.

I grabbed a crumpled piece of paper from the trash can near the desk and smoothed it out. "Time is up, Wayne." I read. "Now it's personal." I looked at Boyd. "Do you think that's a threat?"

"Sounds more like what comes after the threat."

I glanced at a calendar on the wall. "The calendar has Wayne's handwriting. It doesn't match the note. He didn't write this."

"Now what?"

"I'm not sure. Let's hurry and check out the rest of the house, then go talk to Jett."

We checked everything quickly, and right as we were about to leave, I saw something glint on the floor in the kitchen. I went over and squatted. A long silver hoop earring sat on the tile floor.

"Chelsea's earring. Why would Chelsea have been here?"

"Are you sure it's hers?"

"No, but it looks just like the ones she wore last night." I snapped a picture of the earring. I didn't want to disturb all the evidence.

She'd clearly hated Wayne. But enough to... what? It didn't make sense. She wasn't strong enough to drag a body, but that earring didn't get there by itself.

We opened the back door. Boyd had been right. Jett was standing outside with a worried expression.

"There's blood in his office, a threatening note, and one of Chelsea's earrings."

Jett's frown deepened.

"What can we do?" Boyd asked. "We can't call the police and tell them we walked into the house."

I chewed the inside of my cheek. "I'll call and tell them I went into Wayne's house to feed his snake. He did invite me."

Jett nodded. "That might work."

I called the police again, and the same woman answered. She sounded annoyed when I explained it was me again.

"Let me transfer you to Detective Madson," she said.

"Hello? Detective Madson," a deep voice said.

"Hi, my name's Ivy Clark."

"You're the one who called about Wayne."

"Yes. I was supposed to meet him at his house today. He was going to let me help feed his snake. He wasn't there, and there's blood in his office and a note that might be considered threatening."

"Miss Clark, Wayne is always up to something strange. We end up at his house at least once a month, and it's never for a valid reason."

"But the blood—"

"With Wayne, it could be anything. I'm sure he's fine. He does things to get attention."

"He was at my parents' house last night acting a little odd."

"That's not surprising."

"Something was wrong with him."

"Also not surprising. Leave it alone, and he'll probably be back tomorrow."

"There's an earring on the floor of his kitchen. It belongs to one of the neighbors."

"That's not a crime."

I frowned. "If he's hurt or worse, and you don't do anything, you're going to have to live with the fact that you didn't help."

He sighed. "Fine. I'll come take a quick look around."

"Thank you." I hung up. "I don't think I'm going to like Detective Madson."

Chapter 8

I paced across the living room floor and occasionally muttered something to myself. If the detective didn't call back soon, I was going to explode.

"Come sit," Jett said. "You're going to make yourself crazy." He sat on the couch watching me.

I dropped onto the couch and slumped against it. "Do you think they'll do anything?"

"It's hard to say. They probably will if it's really blood."

I pulled off my shoe and tossed it to the floor. I hadn't realized my feet were getting sore. Now I would probably have blisters. I should have taken them off a long time ago.

"I should go change," I said, not moving.

"Do you have to?" Jett teased, scooting closer. "I've enjoyed watching you pace around in that dress." Jett had already gone back to his jeans and button-up shirt. He put his arm over my shoulders, and I leaned into him.

"Why am I so stressed?" I asked. "I don't even know Wayne that well, and I think he's weird."

"Because you're a good person."

I blew a curl out of my eye. "Do you think they'll call me back?"

"Probably. Things like this take a long time. The cop car is still outside, so at least you know they're doing something."

"I guess that's true."

A knock on the door had me running to answer. I could hear Jett walking behind me. I threw open the door to see a tall man with dark brown hair, wearing a suit.

"Ivy Clark?" he asked.

"Yes."

"I'm Detective Madson. We've looked around the house, and I don't think that there's a problem. We will have the blood tested to see if it matches Wayne, and we will try to contact him."

"How can you say there's no problem?"

"There's no sign of a struggle. Nothing but the blood. Knowing Wayne, he probably cut himself."

"He's a neat freak. He would have cleaned it up. And his bed wasn't made." I realized I sounded crazy, but that was all I had. "And what about the earring? That belongs to the neighbor across the street. She didn't leave the party until hours after he did. Why would she go there?"

"Perhaps she's like you and she wanted to be a good neighbor."

"She's not like that."

"Let us do our job, alright?"

I nodded. I could tell he was annoyed at me and just wanted to leave. "Fine." I closed the door and spun around, almost slamming into Jett.

"He's not going to do anything," I said.

"Maybe not. Let them test the blood and see what happens."

I took a deep breath. There wasn't anything else I could do. We went back to the living room and sat. Creepers had come down and curled up in the corner of a chair. He enjoyed my parents' house. There were lots of soft, cozy places.

I took the remote and turned on the TV. I didn't care what was on. I picked at my fingernail while I thought.

"Does anyone know where Wayne works?" Jett asked. "Could he be working, and you're upset for nothing?"

I opened my mouth to argue but stopped. What if he was just at work? But no—something about the timing, the note, the blood didn't sit right. I'd learned to trust my instincts, and right now they were screaming. Wayne wouldn't leave his office in a mess. He was neat.

"No one's going to convince me Chelsea went to hang out with Wayne. I should go talk to her." I stood, but Jett pulled me onto his lap.

"I saw Chelsea pull away when you were talking to the detective." He wrapped his arms around me and pressed his cheek to mine. "I've seen you gung-ho about a case before, but not like this."

"This is different. Wayne might not be dead. There isn't a body. That makes it more time sensitive. And if something happened to him, I didn't help him even though he asked me to."

He sighed. "I guess you're right." He kissed my cheek. "I'll go figure out where he works and see if he was in today."

⚘

I opened the door to find Chelsea on my porch.

"Hi," she said, flashing a smile. "Hey, I was wondering if you found an earring here after the party? I lost one, and I can't seem to find it anywhere."

I stared at her, wondering what to say. "Umm, I don't think so. We've cleaned and no one's said anything."

"Dang. It was my favorite."

Her tone was casual, but her eyes didn't quite match. They darted toward the street, then back to me. Nervous? Or just annoyed I hadn't handed over the earring?

"I'll keep an eye out."

"Do you know what's going on with Wayne? My mom said the police were there for over an hour."

"He's missing." Jett had called Wayne's office and found that he had taken the next few days off and wasn't planning to go back until after Christmas.

"Missing? He was at the party last night, and he lives alone. Who would think he was missing? I thought they waited like, three days to worry about stuff like that."

I shrugged. "Did you go to Wayne's last night? I did hear something about an earring they found."

She blinked twice. "Why would I ever go to Wayne's? That guy is a nutjob."

"So you weren't over there?"

"No. I've only been there once, and it was when he first moved in. It was before we knew he was odd. It only took about five minutes before we realized we shouldn't have gone over to meet him."

"Does he have any friends?"

"How should I know? I'm not friends with him. I've never seen a car over there, so my guess is no."

She didn't look guilty. That earring had to be hers. I'd gotten a good look at them at the party. At least at one of them. Had she been wearing two? It was possible she lost it earlier. I hadn't paid enough attention.

"How serious are things with your fiancé?" she asked, trying to look past me.

My eyes narrowed. Had she really just asked that? "Pretty serious. That's why we're getting married."

"Hmm. Well, let me know if you find the earring."

"I will. Hey, do you want to know something weird? I never knew your mom dated Frank until yesterday."

She arched her eyebrow. "Seriously? I don't remember a time they weren't dating. They fight like cats and dogs, but they always end up back together."

"Interesting. I wonder how I missed it."

"You know my mom. She's not overly affectionate. She would never act lovey in front of anyone. I feel bad for Frank. He's usually the one who gets the short end of everything. He can hold his temper for a long time. He explodes eventually, but the eruptions are few and far between. My mom's like an active volcano."

"That's too bad."

"I've learned to stay out of her way. I don't know why she became a teacher or a principal. I'm glad I never had to be in her school. Let me know if you find the earring. I have to go."

"See you."

I closed the door and leaned against it. Maybe I was reading too much into her visit. But something about her timing and the smooth way she denied being at Wayne's made my neck prickle.

I pulled out the mixer and began a batch of brownies. Jett and Boyd were helping my dad with something in the garage, and my mom had an appointment, so I had time to bake.

While the brownies were in the oven, I pulled out my phone and went to my email. My heart pounded when I saw an email from Wayne. It was from last night. I opened it and held my breath.

Hello Ivy,

Something is wrong. I think the eggnog I got was poisoned. Not only that but I think there's someone in my house. If I turn up dead, please find the perpetrator and make sure they go to prison.

Regards,

Wayne

P.S. Look into Frank, Lillith, and Chelsea. I've learned things they'd rather die than have get out.

"Are you serious, Wayne?" I said out loud. "What do you know?" I ran a hand over my face and read it again. Couldn't he give me a clue?

I dialed Brian's number. He was the most helpful librarian I'd ever known, and he knew how to get answers.

"Hello, Ivy."

"Hi, Brian."

"How's the vacation?"

"About the same as most of my life."

He chuckled. "That bad, huh?"

"My parents' neighbor is missing, and there's blood in his house."

"Oh no. How can I help?"

"The police don't think it's a problem. Before he disappeared, he sent me an email telling me he thinks someone poisoned him. He also told me he suspects it's one of the three neighbors. He said he knows something about them."

"Hmm," Brian said. "If you tell me their names and anything you know about them, I can see if I can dig up anything. If you have birthdays, that's helpful."

"Thanks, Brian. I know one of their birthdays, but not the others." Chelsea always had big parties and always bragged about being born on Leap Day.

"Let me grab a pen. Okay, shoot."

I gave him all the information I could think of. "Do you think that will be enough?"

"It's hard to say. It depends on how deep of a secret they have and why it's a secret. If you can text me their addresses, that might help with any records."

"Okay, I will. I owe you." I would never be able to pay Brian back for everything he's helped me with. "Are you at the library?"

"No. I'm in Silver Hollow, Nebraska."

"Oh, wow. Wait, is that the place you were going to help people start a library?"

"Yep. I just got here yesterday."

"I don't want to bother you. I can figure this out on my own."

"No, no," Brian said. "I'm happy to help. Right now, the library is a mess and in the planning phase. It's going to take slow, steady work."

"What are the people like who you're helping? It was someone's sister who needed help, right?"

He was quiet for a moment. "Yeah, she's not what I expected. I was picturing an older retired woman who needed a hobby."

"And she's not?"

"No. She's in her mid-thirties and dresses to host a soiree or a gala, not run a library."

"Huh. That's strange."

"I think her rich brother wanted to throw her into a job, then he can ditch her and feel like he did all he could to help her. He can't see the flaws in his plan, but I sure can. He doesn't understand that libraries don't make money.

"He's setting her up to fail, and he doesn't realize it, and he won't listen. I'm not going to let that happen, though. When you have some time, I might need to pick your brain about running the diner. We might put a small bakery in the library so she can make money."

"I'd love to help."

"Thanks. I'll do some quick searches and get back to you."

"Great. Talk to you later."

I hung up, then went to my mom's computer to print out the email. The black ink on the page felt heavier than it should. I read the word "poisoned" again and again, and the casual way he'd said "if I turn up dead." This wasn't a joke. And if it was, it was a sick one. I'd swing by the police station and hope it'd prompt Detective Madson to investigate things more carefully.

Chapter 9

"Don't let go," my dad said from halfway up the ladder.

I kept my hands steady against the ladder legs. "I have it." My dad thought the tree needed one more string of lights. It didn't, but arguing with my dad about Christmas lights was pointless. I'd learned that years ago.

"That's not going to make you win," Frank said from the sidewalk. He flashed his award-winning grin.

My dad turned. "I could win without them, but they add a nice touch."

"You think this mess you've got is going to win?"

"Sure. It's better than the mess you have across the street."

I shook my head. Frank and my dad were like this every year. It used to drive my mom crazy, but now she avoids them when they're outside.

"I think Wayne messed with my decorations," Frank said. "He claims it wasn't him, but he was out there holding a broken piece."

My dad nodded and climbed down from the ladder. "Have you seen Wayne since the party?"

"Nope. The police came over and asked if I'd seen him. I'm sure he's off doing something odd."

"Like what?" I asked.

"With Wayne, who knows? He left me a note a couple of weeks ago that said he knows my family secret. I don't actually have a family secret, so I'm a little confused. I know it was him because I saw him on my doorbell camera."

My eyes narrowed as I thought. "I wonder what he could mean?"

"I don't know. I figured it was a generic note he was leaving for multiple people. All families have secrets, so maybe he thinks he'll get lucky and he can blackmail someone or something."

My mind raced through every town rumor I could remember about Frank. He was a mellow guy until Lillith pushed him past his limits. Was there something darker? If Wayne was bluffing, it was a weird move, but what if he wasn't?

"Are you sure you don't have any secrets he could use?"

He rubbed his chin. "Nothing that would be bad enough to make me pay him to keep it quiet. Even if I did, I would tell him he can go ahead and tell people, and I'd turn him in to the police for blackmail. Of course, I can't prove he was going to blackmail me. He might just be crazy."

My dad looked at Wayne's yard. "He's delusional if he thinks his house is going to win. His decorations are a mess."

I wouldn't tell my dad that his usually were as well. This year was better, but I'd never give him an award for decorating.

Frank and my dad kept talking, so I snuck off into the house. I needed to get to the bottom of this. I shouldn't be out hanging Christmas lights.

I went upstairs and listened at Jett's door. I peeked in. He was lying on the bed with his eyes closed. Creepers was at his side. "Jett?"

His eyes opened, and he lifted his head. "Hey."

"Bored?"

"Maybe a little."

"Do you want to go check out Wayne's office?"

He sighed. "Not especially."

I went over and sat on the bed. "But you're bored."

"I'm not used to having spare time, and I'm not sure what to do with it."

"I'm trying to help you."

"I can't do a lot without getting myself in trouble. If we were in Muddy Creek, I would have gone to his work already. Here, I could end my entire career by getting involved."

"Right. I keep forgetting you aren't the sheriff everywhere. I'll take Boyd. That won't help with your boredom."

"I'll be fine. Your dad wanted help with something. Creepers is even bored enough to hang out with me."

"I didn't mean to bring you here and keep ditching you." He held out his arm, and I curled up next to him and put my arm over his stomach.

"It's good to be bored every once in a while. It doesn't happen to me a lot. I don't have to be bored. I can get up and do something."

"My mom usually schedules the week of Christmas so tight there's no room to breathe. She's either relaxing or she doesn't want to overwhelm you and Boyd."

Boyd came in. "I'm bored."

I sat up. "Do you want to go snoop in Wayne's office?"

"Yep. Let's go."

I leaned down and kissed Jett. "Are you sure you're okay without us?"

"Yes, but you better be careful. Boyd could get in a lot of trouble if he gets caught snooping. That would look bad as the mayor."

Boyd scratched the skin on his head. "Yeah, but there's a difference between you and me. I'm old and tired. If people gossip about me or kick me out of office, it won't ruin my year."

Jett sat up and smiled. "Going to Wayne's office might. You know he works for the sewer treatment plant, right?"

I tilted my head. "Are you serious? What does he do?"

"He's some sort of inspector."

Boyd chuckled. "I guess someone has to do it. I'm just glad it isn't me."

* * *

Boyd and I stood in front of the sewer treatment plant. I wrinkled my nose. If the odor in the parking lot was any indication, this was going to be a smelly experience.

"Are you sure you want to go in there?" Boyd raised his eyebrows.

"Yes."

"I guess we have to do our duty."

My eyes narrowed as Boyd laughed. Oftentimes, I had no idea what Boyd was going to find funny.

We went into the building and scanned the lobby. The stink was worse in here. I could hear running water coming from somewhere, and the hum of machinery.

A man at a desk glanced up. "What?"

I raised my eyebrow. I hadn't expected a warm welcome, but maybe a *Hello, can I help you?*

"We're looking for Wayne Wright. Is he in?"

"Don't know. I'm not his sitter. His office is that way." He pointed with his thumb.

"Thanks." We went down the hall where he pointed. I couldn't believe the man didn't care that we wandered through the place.

"Did you know a wainwright is a person who repairs wagons?" Boyd asked as we passed some doors. "I think Wayne chose the wrong job."

I was only slightly listening. The smell was so bad, I was trying not to gag. We came to a door with Wayne's name on it and pushed it open. It was empty. An old computer sat on a desk with a notebook beside it. The desk didn't have any drawers, and there was nowhere else to stash anything in the small room.

I picked up the notebook and frowned. Someone had written *evidence* on the front in black marker.

"What's inside?" Boyd asked.

I opened it. In Wayne's handwriting, it said, *Who is after me???!!!* I showed it to Boyd.

"People who use that many punctuation marks are always a little disturbed," he said.

I didn't want to admit it, but the tone of the notebook gave me chills. It felt less like someone gathering evidence and more like someone building a case in their own head.

I turned the page. "It says, *Frank Weller is the most likely, but is he a killer?*"

"Hmm."

"*Killer* is underlined three times." I turned to the next page. "Here it says, *Lillith has the most to lose.*"

I handed the notebook to Boyd. He turned the page. "*Chelsea hates me. Ignorance doesn't equal innocence.*"

I shook my head. "I wish he could make more sense."

Boyd nodded. "The next page says, *The screening area is ideal.* The rest of the notebook is blank."

"What's the screening area?"

"No clue."

I blew some hair from my face in frustration. "Is there a screening area here?"

"Could be. I've never studied sewer stuff."

We went back out to the man at the desk.

"Hi," I said. "Does this place have a screening room?"

He looked up and rolled his eyes. "Of course it does."

I would ignore the fact that he didn't want to talk to us. "What's it for?"

"It's where the big garbage in the waste is removed. Sticks and stuff."

"Can we see it?"

His forehead creased. "Why would you want to see it?"

"Research?"

He sighed and stood. "I'll show you, but only for a minute." We followed him back through a musty hallway.

He opened a door, and we walked out onto a metal walk-way that went over flowing waste. The smell in the other area was nothing compared to this. My stomach rolled, and I reminded myself I had to breathe.

"Oh gross," I muttered as I looked down into the waste-filled area. Some type of grate was catching big branches and garbage that flowed through. My nose burned, and I could feel the banana I had eaten before we came trying to come back up. I'd never encountered a smell so foul.

"It's not pretty," the man agreed. "You get used to it."

I nodded and ran from the room. I went back through the hall, the lobby, and out the door. I took a deep breath of air that might not be fresh, but it was better than the air inside. Boyd came out behind me.

"I guess we're done here?"

"Yep."

He chuckled. "Not the most pleasant place."

"We're going to make the car smell."

"Without a doubt."

We climbed into the rental car, and I wondered how much extra they would charge us for making it stink. I rolled down all the windows, and we drove silently. I kept swallowing, trying to get the gross feeling swirling around inside me to settle.

My dad and Jett were outside doing something to one of the big gingerbread men.

I got out of the car and slammed the door. I'd leave the windows down to air things out.

"I'm off to the shower," Boyd said, hurrying across the lawn.

Jett came over and opened his arms. "How did it go?" He had almost reached me when he frowned and stepped back. He sniffed.

I sighed. "I know."

"Oh, man. I've been camping a lot, and I've never smelled an outhouse that bad."

"Thanks a lot."

He smiled. "I love you no matter how you smell. But I think I'll keep my distance until you shower."

I cringed. "I almost threw up."

"I'm not surprised."

"If our only clues are there, I'm going to fail. There's no way I can go back to that smelly place. I don't know how anyone works there."

"They must get used to it." He took another step back. "You might want to go—"

"I know." I marched past him, then hurried through the house to my bathroom.

I couldn't think of why Wayne would think the screening room was good for anything. Nothing was coming to me. Wayne thought he knew something, but did he? Unless he thought something or someone could disappear in there.

I shook the idea away. Even Wayne wouldn't fake his own death just to make a point. Right? Had what he'd known been his downfall?

I sighed as I turned on the shower. I might have to burn my clothing. I couldn't imagine that smell coming out.

"Ignorance isn't innocence," I mumbled to myself. What could that mean, and how could it apply to Chelsea? Why was Wayne so obsessed with other people's lives? Was he only obsessed with the people across the street? The notebook hadn't mentioned anyone else.

Chapter 10

Every time I woke up at night, I could smell sewage. I was sure most of it was in my head, but it was giving me weird dreams. I'd washed my hair three times and thrown my clothes out. Jett told me the smell was gone, but I wasn't sure whether he was trying to be polite. I spent a lot of the night tossing and turning as my mind grasped for any kind of direction in Wayne's disappearance.

At five, my eyes popped open. Someone needed to take care of Ginger. She probably needed water and possibly food. There was no way I would touch a snake, but that didn't mean I couldn't fill her water bowl. I jumped up and pulled on my purple robe. My bare feet slapped against the tile hallway.

When I got downstairs, Boyd was sitting at the table with a mug in front of him.

"I need to go check on Wayne's snake." I told him.

Boyd nodded and stood. He wore a T-shirt and plaid pajama bottoms. We went to Wayne's back door, and it took me until we opened the door to realize I didn't put on slippers or shoes. Boyd had house shoes that matched his pajamas.

"My life has been a lot less boring since I met you," Boyd said.

I laughed. "I bet."

"I had no meaning before. I bet I live longer, just for knowing you."

"Glad I could help."

"Of course, I might die earlier because trouble seems to follow you."

I smiled. "Come on." We went to Wayne's room and looked in at the snake enclosure. The water dish was full. "I don't know how to tell if she needs to eat. I bet she does because I was supposed to go watch Wayne feed her."

"Does he have frozen mice?"

"I don't know."

"I bet he does. I'll go look in the freezer."

I cringed at the thought of frozen mice in a freezer used for food. Boyd left the room, and I looked around. Wayne was so neat that any evidence would be obvious. His neatly made bed didn't have the slightest wrinkle.

Boyd came in with something in his hand. I didn't want to see what was inside.

"If she's hungry, we need to thaw this first."

"Why?"

"You can't give a snake a frozen mouse."

"How do you know?"

"I was a farmer."

I tilted my head. "And as a farmer, you thawed mice to feed to snakes?"

He laughed. "Not exactly. I had a pet snake once."

"How do we thaw it?"

"Leave it out for a while."

I got on my hands and knees and looked under the bed. I wasn't sure what I expected to find. There wasn't the smallest dust bunny. Next, I checked the closet. I wasn't sure how thorough Detective Madson had been since he didn't want to do anything in the first place. Everything was neat and orderly in the closet, except for one dirty blue-and-white Nike running shoe. I couldn't imagine Wayne running.

My eyes scanned the room. "I hate to say it, but I wonder if we should be looking for a body."

Boyd nodded. "I've been thinking that all along. If he thought he'd been poisoned, whoever did it must have come in after the party. That blood didn't come from being poisoned, unless he fell because of it and hurt himself."

"I can't believe the police aren't taking this more seriously."

"I can. Wayne's a character. They're tired of dealing with him."

"Wayne thought the eggnog was poisoned. Frank had Wayne's eggnog at one point. Anyone could have tampered with it because he left it outside."

"The earring is what's suspicious to me. If it belonged to your friend, she would have had to be here." Boyd opened the snake enclosure and stuck his hand in. Ginger wrapped around his hand. I shivered.

"Don't let her escape."

Boyd grinned. "You think she's going to jump down and run away?" His smile faded. "I think she already ate. There's a bit of a lump inside her."

"If someone had come in after the party to feed Ginger, it had to be someone who knew their way around snakes. Or someone who'd been in the house before. Like Chelsea. But why would she lie about it?"

I tapped my finger against my lip. "Wayne told me someone was feeding her. He couldn't figure it out."

Boyd put the snake back. "That makes no sense. Why would someone break into Wayne's house to feed his snake?"

I shrugged. "He thought they were playing mind games with him."

"If they killed him, why would they come back to feed her?"

"I dunno. Maybe they like snakes?"

"I'll go put the mouse back. She's not going to need it if she was fed recently."

"But what if she wasn't?"

"I'm pretty sure she was. We can come back and feed her tomorrow. That way, she'll have time to digest if she did, and if she didn't, it won't hurt her to go a little longer."

"What are you two doing?" Jett asked from the doorway.

"Checking on the snake," I explained.

"In your pajamas?"

I grinned. "It looks that way."

"Did you check on it?"

"Yes. She's fine."

"Good, let's go back."

We went to my parents' house and sat at the table. My dad was frying bacon in a skillet. My mom sat at the table with a mug in her hand.

"Morning," she said.

I yawned. "Good morning."

"Why were you outside in your robe?"

"We were checking on Wayne's snake."

"I wonder if we should bring her over here?"

"Not yet," my dad said. "Not until we're sure Wayne isn't coming back."

My phone rang. Brian's name came up. "Hi, Brian," I said.

"Hello. I found some weird stuff for you."

I perked up. "Oh yeah? What is it?"

"It turns out Frank Weller and Lillith Rodriguez were married thirty-four years ago."

I put a hand to my forehead. "What? They're married?"

"They were married. They got divorced less than three years later."

"Weird. I wonder why."

"It said *irreconcilable differences*. Frank had finished college but still worked a low-paying job. The house he lives in belonged to his uncle. Lillith was a senior in college at the time."

"How long was she in the house she's in now?"

"She moved in a year after the divorce with her baby daughter, Chelsea."

"Why move in next to your ex?"

"No idea."

"This is a lot to take in."

"I tried to find information on Chelsea's dad. There wasn't a lot. His name was Kevin Matthews. His name was on the birth certificate, but that's about it. He never paid any child support or had anything to do with Chelsea or Lillith after the birth. I wouldn't be shocked to find he didn't know about Chelsea."

"All there is about him is the name?"

"Yes. There are too many Kevin Matthews to pin down a specific one without more information. Sorry I couldn't get more."

"No, this is great. Thanks, Brian. You're the best."

"Any time."

I hung up. Everyone in the room looked contemplative.

"I can't believe those two were married," my mom said.

"You could hear that?"

Boyd laughed. "Even I could hear. I don't think of Brian as a loud person. He must have been excited."

"That could be the secret Wayne found out about."

"Would that be enough of a secret to blackmail someone over?" I asked. "I mean, they've been dating off and on since then, and it seems I'm the only person who didn't know that."

"It's hard to tell," my dad said. "Maybe Wayne would think so. He's a little... peculiar."

"I wish I was still good enough friends with Chelsea to ask her some things. I remember her telling me she didn't know her dad, but she didn't share details."

"We should be planning a wedding, not trying to figure out the way Wayne thinks."

Boyd nodded. "Are you two ever going to come up with a date? I thought you'd be married months ago."

I hugged myself. "The thought of being married in the winter makes me feel... cold."

"You could get married in Arizona," my mom suggested.

I shook my head. "I love Muddy Creek. I want to be around the friends I've made there."

"You don't have to get married outside in the snow," Boyd said. "The church has heating."

But even as we joked and planned, I kept thinking about Wayne. What if all his weirdness had been real fear? What if someone really did want to shut him up?

My mom grinned. "Then you can spend the rest of the cold winter snuggled up with Jett."

"It sounds good to me," Jett said, taking a sip from a cup. "Just you and me, sitting in the window seat watching the snow."

"Don't forget about Creepers and Conan," Boyd said.

Jett frowned. "Don't ruin my fantasy, Boyd."

I could picture it—with or without the animals.

Creepers wandered into the kitchen and meowed.

"You insulted him," I told Jett.

He grinned. "He's going to have to get used to sharing. That cat is spoiled."

"Most of that's Boyd's fault."

Boyd shrugged. "Someone has to do it."

"How did you raise animals without spoiling them all?" I asked.

Boyd shrugged. "There were too many on the farm to let them get too spoiled. I did have some favorite animals. I hid a raccoon when I was a teenager. He bit me one day, and I had to tell my parents. They made me get a rabies shot. Those things are brutal. I stuck with domesticated animals after that."

My dad put a plate of bacon on the table, then went back for eggs. It felt weird not to spend so much of my day baking. I love the diner, but sometimes it's nice not to think about it so much. I knew it was in good hands with José and Carrie.

"I can't believe the police aren't taking anything seriously," I said. I couldn't seem to stay off the subject of Wayne for more than a few minutes. "Even after the email he sent me, they don't seem concerned."

Jett swallowed a bite of eggs. "I understand to an extent. Some individuals consume a significant amount of police resources and time. It gets frustrating when you know they don't actually need help. It sounds like that's what's happened with Wayne. It's still odd they aren't doing much now that he's missing."

"Do you think they'll at least have the blood tested?"

He nodded. "I bet they're doing more than you think. You just won't know because they aren't going to tell you."

I kept going over the clues—blood, the snake, the notebook, the earring. It was almost too clean. Too conveniently mysterious.

"That's frustrating."

"No one around here knows about the famous Ivy Clark," Boyd teased.

"Unless they're Wayne. It's a little weird he started an online group about me."

"Sorry," my mom said. "We shouldn't have told him anything about you."

"It's not your fault. You didn't know he would be so strange about it."

"Everyone, hurry up and eat," my mom said. "We have a Christmas concert this afternoon, and then tonight, we'll go caroling."

My dad and I let out a synchronized groan.

"Oh, stop that. I know deep down you both love it."

I could tolerate the concert, but I hated caroling. I'd never seen anyone look anything but awkward during caroling. Who wanted to open their door to a bunch of people staring at you while they sang? Not me. Everyone wore a phony smile and hoped it would end soon. Sure, we left them with a plate of goodies, but that didn't take away from the uncomfortable feeling I always had.

"I'm not sure anyone wants to hear me sing," Boyd said. "I'm not tone deaf, but I'm right next door to it."

"I won't force you to come," my mom said, "but we would love to have you. No one cares what it sounds like."

My mom could say that confidently because she has a great singing voice. I wasn't terrible, but I wasn't good either.

"Can't I make the goodies, and you and Dad sing?" I asked hopefully.

My mom smiled. "You can make the goodies *and* sing."

I looked at Jett. "I'm thirty years old and still getting bossed around by my mom."

He grinned. "I'm not sure that ever ends."

My dad nodded. "Sometimes it's best to just go with it."

Chapter 11

I watched Frank take a shovel from his truck and carry it into his backyard. We'd gotten back from the Christmas concert, and the oven was full of cinnamon rolls for caroling. What could Frank be doing with a shovel? I pulled on my shoes and quietly went out the front door. I snuck around Frank's house and peeked into the backyard.

Frank was in the middle of the garden digging. He didn't seem to care that he was ruining plants. But it wasn't just random digging—he was digging a hole. The kind that looked measured. That seemed suspicious to me. I couldn't stay hidden here forever, and right now, nothing was happening worth mentioning to anyone. Just a man in his garden. Killing his plants. I went back home, planning to come back when he wasn't there.

When I got inside, Jett was pacing across the living room.

"What's wrong?" I asked.

"Ledford just called. Someone stole my truck and totaled it."

I frowned. "We have bad luck with vehicles."

"Ledford said it was deliberate."

"I'm sorry. You love that truck."

He shrugged. "Not as much as I did at first. I've thought a few times I'd rather have a regular truck again. That doesn't make it less annoying. The insurance will pay for it, but if someone did it deliberately, I need to know why."

Jett had a Cybertruck that Boyd bought for him. I thought it looked ridiculous, but Jett and Boyd seemed to think it was great.

"There are probably lots of people who might want to get back at you for tickets or busting them."

"Too many. I'm not sure I could narrow it down. Ledford told me he's looking into it."

I wanted to tell him he could go home and investigate it, but I didn't want to spend Christmas without him.

"Don't worry. I'm not going anywhere," he said like he'd read my mind. "Ledford and the others are capable. I just need to think."

I nodded and went to the kitchen so he could have time. Sometimes I wished Jett had a quiet, normal job where people didn't target him. I could understand why he got upset when I got myself into danger.

The timer beeped, and I pulled a pan of cinnamon rolls out of the oven. They smelled delicious.

"Chelsea's at the door," my mom said, coming in and opening the fridge.

My mouth turned down. I wondered what she could want. I went and found her standing in the entryway.

"Hi," I said.

"Hey. So I found something in my mom's room. I know you do all that investigating stuff, and I figure with the questions you were asking that you're trying to find Wayne."

"What did you find?"

She fiddled with a ring on her finger. "It was a note. It said something like *Secrets can't stay secrets forever.* I left it where I found it."

"You didn't ask your mom about it?"

"No. She doesn't like it when I get into her business. She's been a lot more stressed lately. I wonder if someone was blackmailing her."

"It sounds possible."

"Do you think it's related to Wayne?"

"I'm not sure. Can I ask you something?"

She shrugged.

"Has your mom ever been married?"

"No. She came close a time or two."

"To marrying Frank?"

"Yeah. I thought they should. In reality, they are a terrible couple, but he's nice and she isn't. My home life might have been better."

"Why do you still live with her?"

"I don't know. Apartments are expensive."

"Do you know what happened to your dad?"

"No. My mom doesn't talk about that at all, and she gets mad if I ask. I thought about doing a DNA test, but that would make her freak out. I still think about doing one occasionally. Not that I need a dad at this point in my life. It's good to know where you come from, though."

"You have no clue who might have sent the note?"

"None. The night of the party, my mom came home late. She seemed upset. I didn't ask because she hates that. She was shaking, and she went and washed her hands and drank two glasses of water. She muttered to herself, then went to talk to Frank."

"Anything else?"

She rubbed a hand over her face. "I have no proof, but I'm worried Wayne might have been blackmailing her. I think my mom killed Wayne."

"Why would you think that?" I asked carefully.

She hesitated. "She's just... not herself. And she was so weird about that note."

But something about the way she avoided my eyes made me wonder—was she afraid of her mom, or covering for herself?

"I saw someone in Wayne's house," my dad said. "Upstairs, walking past the window."

I dropped the paper plates I was going to use for the cinnamon rolls. "Was it Wayne?"

"It was just a shadow."

"I'm going over."

Jett's eyes pierced mine. "To knock on the front door?"

"Yes."

"Nothing else?"

"Nothing."

"I'll come with you."

He took my hand, and we went next door. We knocked several times, but the house stayed quiet.

"Do you think it was Wayne?" I asked.

Jett frowned. "I don't know. This whole thing is so odd."

Lillith came marching across the street. "Is Wayne home yet?"

"No."

She mumbled something.

"Where did you go after my parents' party?" The question slipped out before I had time to decide whether it was a good one.

Her eyes narrowed. "Why are you asking me that? Chelsea told me you think you're some type of private eye or something. You can't think I have anything to do with Wayne's disappearance."

"It was just a question."

"Yeah? Well, where were you?"

"Cleaning up after the party."

She put her hands on her hips. "Do you have any witnesses?"

"Several."

"Why would I do anything to Wayne?"

"Because he was bothering you. Threatening to tell people things you didn't want them to know."

She twitched, then pushed her braid over her shoulder. "I don't know what you're talking about."

"Wayne told me he had something over on you."

"Why would he say that?"

"No idea."

"Is he spreading that around, or did he only tell you?"

"The police know." I didn't add that they knew and didn't care.

Her face went pale. "What do they know?"

I shrugged. "Just that Wayne knew something about you that you might not want getting out. I don't think they know what he thinks you did."

Her eyes narrowed. "This is ridiculous. If I ever find that man, he's going to be sorry."

"He might be already."

"I don't know what would make you think I did anything. I'm not going to stand here and be insulted." She stormed to her house, and I stared after her.

Jett took my hand, and I jumped. I'd forgotten he was standing there.

"Is that how you always talk to suspects?" he asked.

"I'm not sure. I fly by the seat of my pants most of the time."

"You have intense eye contact. I was about ready to confess to some things."

I smiled sheepishly. "I probably should work on my confrontations. She didn't sound like someone who had killed Wayne."

"That might be a front. She could be scared that you're looking into things."

"Maybe. Frank was digging in his garden earlier."

He groaned and led me toward the house. "I hope I don't find you out at midnight digging in his garden."

I squeezed his hand. "Not at midnight. Chelsea said her mom came home upset after the party. She went to talk to Frank. It had to be pretty late. What if she had a fight with Wayne, killed him, then told Frank? Frank might be trying to hide the body in his garden. He was digging up good plants."

"That's possible. I don't think digging back there is a good idea."

"You would do it if we were in Muddy Creek."

"I would. But we aren't."

We went inside, and the conversation died.

"Who's ready for some caroling?" my mom asked.

I wasn't, but I would do it.

A shattering noise made us all jump.

"Was that upstairs?" I asked.

"Sounded like it," Jett said, running. My mom and I were close behind. Jett took the stairs two at a time and began looking through the rooms. When he got to mine, he stopped. "The window's broken."

I frowned. "Why are people always breaking my windows?"

Jett picked up a rock with a paper taped to it. I shivered. I'd seen that plenty in movies, but never in real life. I moved up to see it.

"Stop," I read. "Stop? Really? That's all they could come up with?"

Jett peeled the paper off and turned it over. "Or you'll be as dead as Wayne."

"What?"

"That's what it says on the other side."

My mom rubbed her lips together. "It might be best if you went back to Kansas early. I don't want you getting hurt."

"I'm not leaving."

"You can't put yourself in danger."

"Muddy Creek might not be any better," Jett said.

I tilted my head and gave him a questioning look.

He sighed. "Ledford called me again. There was a note in my truck. He sent me a picture. The paper matched this," he said, pointing at the cream paper taped to the rock. "The handwriting looks the same, and it was a threat to you, not me."

"How could someone ruin your truck in Kansas and throw something through the window here?"

"It's a short flight. Or multiple people could be involved."

My mom frowned. "I'm going to see if there are available tickets to Disneyland." She left the room.

"Why didn't you tell me about the note in the truck?"

"I was going to, but then your mom called us to help with the cinnamon rolls."

"What did the note say?"

"Nothing worth mentioning. Just threats."

"I need to figure this out before my mom has us on a flight to California."

My phone rang. "It's José," I said, looking at the screen. "Hello?"

"Hey, Ivy." His tone was serious. "Sorry to bother you. I was trying to take care of this without telling you because I don't want to ruin your vacation."

"What is it?"

"Someone graffitied the back of the diner. It happened last night. I was going to have it painted over, but it's too cold to paint."

"Does Ledford know?"

"Yeah, but he said there's nothing he can do about graffiti. The camera caught someone, but it was dark, and they were wearing black with a ski mask. I wasn't going to tell you, but since you're going to come home and see it, I didn't want it to be a shock. It will be easy to paint over once we get a day that's warm enough."

"Thanks, José." I hung up and turned to Jett. "Someone graffitied the diner."

His frown deepened. "Maybe we should go to California."

"What good will that do?"

"It would take you somewhere safe. Even Kansas would be better than here. At least there, I have the authority to look into it and keep you safe."

"I bet whoever it was flew to Kansas last night and was back before morning. Being in Kansas won't help Wayne."

Jett raked his hands through his hair. "But it will help you. If you're there, whoever is leaving notes would have no reason to continue bothering you."

"Not yet." But I couldn't lie. The fear had curled in low and tight. Someone was trying to scare me. And it was working.

"Then I don't want you out of my sight."

"How will that work? You can't get involved. You said so yourself. More than once."

"I'd rather have you than my job."

Chapter 12

"You guys are all ridiculous," I said, glaring across the living room at Boyd. He was on the recliner with his blanket and pillow, and I was lying on the couch with Jett's arms around me. My dad was in the middle of the room, pumping up an air mattress for him and my mom to sleep on.

"If we sleep like this, I know you aren't sneaking out at night to do anything dangerous," Jett said.

"And safety in numbers," my mom said, carrying in a fuzzy blanket. She grabbed it by the corners and flicked it with her wrists, letting it billow down over me and Jett. "If someone comes for you, we're all here."

"I won't be able to sleep. If I move at all, I'm going to fall off the couch," I complained.

Jett squeezed me. "Nope. I've got you."

"Once you fall asleep, you won't."

Boyd chuckled. "Stop complaining, Ivy. We're just keeping you safe. Besides, your room has a broken window."

"It's taped."

"And no one can take tape off?"

I let out a frustrated breath. I wanted to go dig in Frank's backyard. I might be able to slip past one person, but probably not four. I could go tomorrow while Frank was at work, but I would be exhausted from trying not to fall all night.

"It could be worse," Boyd said.

"Yep," Jett agreed. "I could be on the recliner, and you could be cuddled up with Boyd."

My dad and Boyd laughed.

"I'll turn on a movie," my mom said, grabbing the remote. "Then everyone can fall asleep when they're ready."

Creepers came in and jumped on Boyd's chest and curled up. Boyd stroked his fur, and I could hear his purring from clear across the room.

I wasn't in the mood to watch a movie. Results were what I needed, not sleep. We only had a few more days left in Arizona. If we hadn't figured it out by then, we might never. I turned and buried my face into Jett's chest and closed my eyes. This wouldn't work. My rear was only halfway on. I would prefer the air mattress, but my parents wouldn't fit together on the couch.

"Can't we sleep on the floor?" I muttered. "I'll never fall asleep like this."

I was wrong. That was the last thing I remembered thinking. My next coherent thought happened when I slammed into the floor. I frowned and sat up. The TV was dim, and all I could hear was the sound of Boyd and my dad snoring.

I stood and looked at Jett. One arm was over his face, and he was breathing deeply. My fall hadn't woken anyone. I tiptoed to the mudroom, pulled on my shoes, and went into the garage. I closed the door quietly and looked for a shovel.

"What are you doing?" Boyd asked.

I jumped. "Boyd!" I whisper-yelled. "You just about gave me a heart attack."

He grinned. "Are we digging up Frank's garden?"

"Yes." I handed him a shovel and grabbed my own. We went out the garage door and crept across the street and into Frank's backyard. We went to the corner garden. The light from the back porch made it possible to see the ground.

"At least he made it obvious where he dug," Boyd said, looking at the dirt that had been turned over. "It looks like he killed off his bean plants. The carrots were saved."

I started digging. The less time we spent here, the less likely we would be seen.

Boyd whistled as he dug. "Hey," I whispered. "We're trying to be quiet."

"Right." He went back to digging quietly. "I'm not sure there's anything here. The dirt is only loose on the top. After a foot, it's more solid. That tells me it hasn't been disturbed in a while."

"I can see something," I said, bending down. Something white poked out of the dirt. I used my hands to pull it from the earth. It was a blue-and-white shoe. "There was a shoe like this in Wayne's closet."

Boyd leaned on the shovel handle. "Is there a foot to go with that?"

A chill spread across my body as I studied the ground. I moved the dirt around with my shoe. "I don't see one."

"What's the purpose of burying a shoe? There must be a body down there."

I frowned and looked up at the moon. "Why is there only one shoe?"

"A struggle, maybe?"

"But the other shoe is in the closet. A killer isn't going to stop to put one shoe in a closet after a struggle. And who buries a shoe? I've never been so baffled by a case. The other shoe in his closet is dirty," I said. "Wayne's a neat freak. There's no way he'd leave it like that unless he wanted someone to notice it—or unless someone else put it there to throw me off."

Boyd got down on his hands and knees and dug at the dirt where the shoe had been. "There has to be something else. If it fell off a body, the foot would be sticking out or close."

The back door opened, and Frank came barrelling out. I couldn't see a point in running. He'd already seen us.

"What are you doing?" he asked, crossing his arms over his blue robe.

"Digging," Boyd said.

Frank's eyes narrowed. "For what?"

"Wayne."

Boyd wasn't helping.

"You think Wayne is buried in my garden? That's ridiculous."

I held up the shoe. "You only buried his shoe?"

Frank blinked at it. "Never seen it before."

He looked again, longer this time—like he was debating something.

"Why were you digging back here yesterday?" I asked.

"My beans were bad. I was turning them over so I can plant something else."

"Like Wayne?" Boyd asked.

He rolled his eyes. "I didn't bury Wayne. Or that shoe."

"Maybe the police should come do some digging," I suggested.

He shrugged. "Sure, why not? Then they can arrest you for trespassing."

"What did Wayne know about you that he didn't want getting out?"

"I have no idea. I'm a boring person. He kept sending me messages saying he knew my secret. He was crazy."

"Did he demand money?"

He shook his head. "No. He just said he knew things. I assumed a demand would come later, but it never made sense. If I had any secrets, I might have been scared."

"No secrets at all? No hidden marriages?"

He frowned. "You know about Lillith?"

I nodded.

"We only keep that a secret because Lillith doesn't want Chelsea to know we were married. I'm not sure why she cares. I wouldn't pay someone money not to let that get out, and I wouldn't kill anyone."

"Why did you get divorced?"

"It's the middle of the night. Is all of this necessary?"

"I have to find out what happened to Wayne."

He sighed. "We didn't have a lot of money. Lillith was still in school, and I had a job without insurance. That can cause a lot of stress in a marriage. Lillith wanted to use government resources to get by, and I didn't. We had a big fight, and she left."

"Why did she move back?"

"She's complicated. I don't think she got over me. She tried. When her relationship with Chelsea's dad ended, I think she panicked and wanted to be close to me again. I helped her with Chelsea and paid for some of her college."

"But you never remarried?"

"Obviously not. Now can I go back to bed?"

"There's still the shoe," I said, holding it up.

"I've never seen it. If it makes you happy, you can dig all night. You won't find anything. Try not to hurt my carrots." He turned and went back to his house.

"I'm calling the police," I said. "Wayne might not be buried here, but it's still odd to find his shoe." I grabbed my phone and made a quick call. Less than ten minutes later, Detective Madson walked into the backyard. He must have just woken up and come right over. He still had pillow lines on his face.

"What's going on, Miss Clark?"

I held up the shoe. "We found Wayne's shoe buried here."

His eyes narrowed. "What would make you dig here?"

"I saw Frank digging here."

"I've been digging," he said. "And do you want to know what I found? Wayne Wright was obsessed with you. He made a fan site. From what I learned, you ignore the law and take it into your own hands. That's not the way we do things here."

"You don't do things here," I argued. "I brought a problem to your attention, and you're ignoring it."

"I'm not. I had the blood in Wayne's house tested. It belongs to him."

"And?"

"And what? He easily could have hurt himself."

"There's blood, and he disappeared. You should be looking for him."

"How do you know that's his shoe? I bet he thought you'd come play detective. And you did."

I took a deep breath. "The other one's in his closet."

"I'm dealing with this. I'll have someone dig here. You stay out of it."

"Someone threw a rock through my window with a note telling me to stop."

His eyes narrowed. "When?"

"Yesterday."

"And you didn't call? That is something I would take seriously. Go home, and I'll call you tomorrow. Don't come over here again."

I nodded and grabbed my shovel and Boyd's. We went back to my parents' garage and returned them.

"Even if there is no body, someone wanted us to find that shoe," Boyd said.

"You think it's a setup?"

"I think someone wants to distract you."

It was possible, but I wasn't sure what to do with that information.

"Sneak back to the recliner," I whispered. Boyd nodded and slipped off his shoes. I took mine off and tiptoed into the living room. Boyd climbed onto the chair and pulled the covers over himself.

Jett had rolled himself into the fetal position, and there was no way I could fit next to him. I sat on the floor near his head and poked him in the nose. He twitched. I poked him again. His eyes opened.

"Hmm?"

"You made me fall," I whispered. It wasn't a lie; it had just been fifty minutes earlier.

He sat up and rubbed his eyes. "Sorry."

"It's okay. I went to Frank's and dug up a shoe."

He yawned. "Ha ha."

I climbed onto the couch and got in Jett's spot. He could be the one to fall off next time.

"I can't be on the end," he said.

"Sure you can." I grabbed him and wrapped my arms around him. "Don't worry. I won't let you fall."

"He'll take you both down," Boyd said.

"Shhh, Boyd," I said. "You're supposed to be asleep."

Jett groaned. "You really did go dig, didn't you?"

"Only because you knocked me on the floor."

He stood and pulled me to my feet. "Trade us places, Boyd."

I grabbed the pillow and blanket, and Boyd came with his bedding. My parents hadn't stirred.

Jett climbed onto the recliner, and I squished next to him, pulling up the blanket.

"You found a shoe?" he asked.

"Yes. It's Wayne's. The other one's in his house. I called the police, and we talked to Frank. I don't think there's a body down there, but I can't figure out why there would be a shoe."

"Go to sleep, and we'll figure it out tomorrow."

"We better. I'm not spending another night like this."

Chapter 13

I hummed a Christmas song as I rolled out sugar cookie dough. The only Christmas cookie cutters my mom had were ninja gingerbread men, and I didn't care enough to go buy more.

The doorbell rang.

"I'll get it," Jett said, standing up from the table. My parents were grocery shopping, and Boyd had gone with them.

I grabbed a cookie cutter and cut out a ninja kicking.

"Hello, Ivy," Lillith said, entering the kitchen.

I stopped humming and looked up. Jett went into the living room, and Lillith stood next to the island where I was working.

"Hi."

"The police have been buzzing around, asking about Wayne."

"Oh." I cut out another ninja.

"It's not very neighborly to sic the police on us."

I frowned. "I didn't send them to you."

"Frank, me, it's the same."

"Hmm?"

"Frank said you found Wayne's shoe in his garden. Now the police are digging everything up. It's a mess. Frank told me you know we were married. I hope you'll keep that to yourself. I don't want Chelsea upset."

"She likes Frank."

"Yes, but she might not if she knew."

"It's strange to keep secrets like that. They always come out."

She pushed her dark brown hair over her shoulder. "But that's my business. I'd like you to stay out of it."

"Not if it's related to Wayne's death."

"I realize you think you're Jessica Fletcher, but you're not. Mind your business."

I cut more cookies. "I don't see how a marriage from so long ago could cause any real problems. It's been decades."

She set her jaw, and her eyes narrowed. "Just leave things alone. I'd hate for something to happen to you."

"Are you threatening me?"

"Of course not. I'm just saying. It's dangerous to get involved in things like this."

"Where's Chelsea's dad?"

"How should I know? I haven't seen him in years."

"He never paid child support?"

"No."

"How did you take care of Chelsea when she was young?"

"There are programs that help single moms."

"You were fortunate to finish your education."

She nodded. "I'm done here. Remember what I said." She swung around and walked purposely away.

"What's she hiding?" Jett asked, coming into the kitchen.

"Were you listening?"

"Yep."

"I have a theory, but I'm not ready to throw it out."

"She's got something keeping her quiet."

I placed the ninja cookies on a baking sheet. "I've always been scared of Lillith. I'm not sure why. When I was little, I thought she was a witch. I was sure she didn't like kids."

"It's always strange who goes into education. I had a few teachers who I was sure were in the wrong profession."

"I wonder if my mom would invite Lillith, Chelsea, and Frank to dinner tonight."

"Why? That sounds awful."

"I'd like to talk to them all together. It might help me make sense of a few things."

"I doubt Lillith will agree to come over."

"Maybe not. But we're running out of time."

Jett nodded. "Okay."

I tilted my head. "Okay?"

He grinned. "What do you want me to say?"

"You don't usually go along with me that easily."

"Well, you aren't asking to go chase someone through a dark alley or anything. Dinner won't hurt anything."

This was one of the most awkward dinners I'd had in a long time. My parents kept trying to start conversations, but Lillith would hardly talk. Chelsea would answer for her, then her mom would glare at her. Frank tried to keep his side of the conversation, but he kept looking awkwardly around.

I was probably as bad as Lillith. I was studying Frank and not adding to the conversation. He'd been my neighbor most of my life, but I'd never spent a lot of time around him. Something was coming together in my mind, but it was taking its sweet time.

"This is really good," Chelsea said, scooping a forkful of potatoes into her mouth.

"Frank is Chelsea's dad," I said. I didn't mean it to come out like that.

Lillith dropped her fork, her eyes wide.

Chelsea's eyes narrowed. "What?"

Frank chuckled. "I wish I was, but I'm not."

"You have the same ears, and your eyes are shaped the same. That's why Wayne was bothering you. He knew somehow."

Lillith glared at me. "That's insane. Her father's name was Kevin Matthews."

"I bet Kevin Matthews doesn't exist."

Boyd shook his head and kept eating.

Lillith laughed. "That's the craziest thing I've ever heard. Candy, you let your girl grow up with too much imagination."

Chelsea was touching her ear and staring at Frank.

My mom shot me a look. I couldn't tell if she was warning me off or just nervous. Jett and my dad both leaned back in their chairs and looked like they were ready to watch a movie.

"What month did you get divorced?" I asked.

Lillith's first glare was nothing compared to this one.

"August," Frank said.

I raised my eyebrow. "And Chelsea was born in February."

Frank's eyes landed on Lillith. "Well?"

"What do you mean, divorced?" Chelsea said. "You two were married?"

Frank nodded, his eyes not leaving Lillith. "It was a long time ago."

"Mom?"

Lillith stood. "This is ridiculous. I don't have to sit here and take this. Come on, Chelsea."

Chelsea didn't move. "I'm not going anywhere until you tell me what happened."

"Do you really want to air out our dirty laundry in front of the neighbors?"

"It's a little late to avoid that. It looks like Ivy knows more about me than I do. Is Frank my dad?"

"Don't be ridiculous."

Frank looked at Chelsea. "We can do a DNA test."

"Why would I lie about this?"

I pushed my plate away. "Because you didn't have the money to have a baby. You wanted to get government help, and Frank didn't. I guess you figured the best thing to do was get divorced and try it on your own."

Lillith swallowed and looked at Frank. "You shouldn't have been so stubborn!"

His eyes narrowed. "You mean it's true?"

She moved her jaw from side to side.

"It's true," Chelsea said. "She only moves her mouth like that when she's being stubborn and doesn't want to admit something."

"Why would Wayne use that as a threat?" Boyd asked.

Jett leaned forward and rested his elbows on the table. "Intentionally lying on a birth certificate is a crime. You could at least get a fine. Possibly face criminal charges. I'm assuming if she did that, she also took advantage of government programs that she might not have been able to if she were still married."

Chelsea crossed her arms. "I'm changing my last name." She wasn't just angry. She was wounded. People didn't always think clearly when their entire life unraveled in an evening.

Lillith rolled her eyes. "Stop being dramatic."

"Frank didn't lie to me all my life! You kept me from having a father and he was right under my nose!"

"Everyone here is assuming a lot. I don't have to explain myself to any of you."

Frank glared. "But you should. If what Ivy said is true, you have a lot of explaining to do. Did you kill Wayne?"

"How could you even think that?"

"They said something about poison in the eggnog. You handed me Wayne's eggnog when he left it outside and told me to give it to him."

"I was only being neighborly."

"You're never neighborly. Especially to Wayne."

"This is the most ridiculous thing I've ever heard. If I killed Wayne, where did his body go? He has to weigh at least three times more than I do. I wouldn't be able to move him a foot, let alone hide him."

I sized up Lillith. She was probably right. Wayne, being dead weight, would be hard for anyone to move, and Lillith was probably five-foot-two and one hundred pounds.

"What have you been doing at his house?" Chelsea asked. "I've seen you sneak back twice since he disappeared."

Lillith gripped the top of the chair. "I was checking to see if he was home."

"I saw you come from the back once."

"What do you do? Sit at home and spy out the window?"

"I shouldn't have washed all the dishes so fast," my mom muttered. "Then the police could have tested his for poison."

I shook my head. "His broke. Remember?"

"Right."

Lillith sneered. "No body, no crime."

"That's not true," Jett said. "People have been convicted without a body turning up before."

Frank rubbed his chin. "I still want to know how Wayne's shoe ended up in my garden."

I looked at the shoe again in my mind. One in the closet, one in the garden. Who would do that? Someone cleaning up a mess... or someone making one?

Lillith crossed her arms. "Don't look at me. Why would I bury a shoe in your yard?"

"To frame me? You didn't tell me I had a daughter. I wouldn't put anything past you."

"I had to leave the marriage. If I hadn't, we wouldn't have had the resources to raise Chelsea. You were too stubborn to get the help we needed."

"That's not true. We weren't rich, but we could have made it. A year after you left, I'd gotten a good job, and I became financially well off. Things might have been tight, but we would have been fine."

Chelsea wiped tears from her cheeks. "I can't believe any of this. I'm going to need therapy."

"I'll pay for it," Frank said. "I'm sorry I wasn't there for you."

"You were," Chelsea said. "You always helped me. I used to wish you were my dad. You paid for my school, and you gave me a cookie every time my mom was on a tirade."

Lillith's teeth cracked because she was grinding them so hard. "I'm not going to sit and be put through this. Sure, I hid some things, but I refuse to be accused of murder. All of these are your accusations without any proof. You show me a body, and then we can talk. And who says Frank didn't do it? The shoe was in his yard."

Jett gave me a look. One I'd seen him use when a suspect pushed too hard, too fast. Lillith was either guilty... or desperate to look like she wasn't.

Frank glared. "You know I didn't do it. I had nothing to hide. You, on the other hand, did."

"Who cares about Wayne? Why are we even discussing him? He was threatening people and into everyone's business. I didn't kill him, but if I did, I would have done everyone a service."

"I'm on my way," a muffled voice said, causing me to jump.

"Who said that?" Lillith demanded.

Jett held up his phone. "Detective Madson. He's been listening in."

The color drained from her face. "I'm not wasting any more time here." She turned and walked from the kitchen.

"Don't make it harder on yourself than you need to," Jett warned.

She peeked back in. "You have no authority here. I checked."

I raised my eyebrow. "Why check if you're innocent?"

Jett shrugged. "I don't have jurisdiction here. If I did, I wouldn't let you leave the house. I'm warning you to be polite. Don't make Detective Madson hunt for you. That will only make you look more guilty and get him angry."

She glared and disappeared into the hallway.

"Well, this is a mess," Chelsea said. "Now what?"

Frank put his hand on her arm. "Why don't you come to my house, and we can have a long talk?"

She nodded, and they left.

We all sat around the table, looking at each other. Except Boyd. He was eating.

My mom twisted her napkin. "I don't doubt Lillith did it, but she's right. There's no way she could move Wayne.

He's a big guy, and Lillith can't even start her lawn mower without help. I've had to go across and do it for her several times."

Jett shrugged. "I've seen some strange things people have done over the years when they're determined."

"Has anyone looked in Wayne's garage?" I wondered. "Is his car there? I can't believe I never checked. What if she went over and he wasn't dead yet? She could have coaxed him into the car and done something. I'm going to check."

Jett grabbed my hand as I stood. "Don't. I think Lillith made Detective Madson listen, finally. I bet he does a more thorough investigation now. He'll check the garage first thing. You don't want him to find you in there."

I sighed and sat back down. "I would do it if we were in Muddy Creek."

He grinned. "I'm sure you would. But I hear the sheriff of Muddy Creek is a bit of a pushover when it comes to certain people."

Chapter 14

Christmas Eve has always been the most exciting day of the year for me. Every year, we make a variety of goodies and watch *A Christmas Carol*. Not just one version, but three. My dad likes every version, so we rotate them every year. The only one we watch every year without fail is the one with Albert Finney, then we all walk around the house singing the songs.

Another thing we do is make a dessert for my mom's friend, who lives a few miles away. We take it to her, and she complains about everything. This year, I was making the dessert, and my parents were going to take it. We didn't want to make Boyd and Jett go, so I got out of that part. I was making a cake with marshmallow fondant, and Jett was making caramel popcorn.

My parents and Boyd were ensuring the house was ready for the judging that would take place later today. I was shocked that my mom agreed to help. She usually avoids anything to do with these things.

I'd never made fondant before, and I probably shouldn't have started when I was giving it to someone. The mixture was so sticky that I wasn't sure I would be able to roll it out. It said to mix it with your hands. It needed more powdered sugar or something because I had a huge glob of fondant wrapped around my hands, and I couldn't put it down.

I went closer to the powdered sugar, but with my hands in this position, I couldn't grab the measuring cup. Pulling my hands apart was only going to make a mess, and I wasn't sure I could do it anyway. I rested my hands near the mixing bowl and looked at the recipe to see if it had any suggestions. When I lifted my hands, a butter knife was stuck to the fondant.

"Seriously?" I muttered, shaking my hands. The knife was there for keeps. "Ugh."

"What's wrong?" Jett asked from the stove.

"The fondant is super sticky. I can't even get it off my hands."

He looked over his shoulder and kept stirring. His eyes sparkled. "It looks like you picked up a knife and a toothpick."

"A toothpick?" I turned my hands around. Sure enough, a toothpick was stuck to the goop. "I give up." I shook my hands harder. "It won't come off."

"Hang on," Jett said. "This is almost done."

Boyd came whistling into the room.

"Hey, can you stir the caramel while I help Ivy for a minute?" Jett asked him.

"Sure." He went over and took the spoon.

Jett came over and grinned at my hands. "I'm not sure how to help."

"Don't touch it, or you'll be stuck too. If you could grab a cup of powdered sugar and dump some on my hands, I might be able to work with it until it isn't sticky."

"Do you want the knife and toothpick off?"

"Yes."

He pulled them off, still smiling. "It will bake off any germs, right?"

"It doesn't bake. The knife was clean. I don't know about the toothpick."

"It's clean," Boyd said. "I dropped a bunch earlier."

Jett dumped powdered sugar onto the fondant, and I kneaded it in. We kept doing that until it was no longer sticky and I could form it into a ball in my hands.

"Thanks," I said.

Jett grinned, then frowned and sniffed. "I think the caramel is burning."

Boyd chuckled. "You said stir. You never said to stop." He took the pan off the heat, and Jett went over to look at it.

"What's burning?" my mom asked, entering the kitchen.

Boyd grinned. "Jett's caramel."

"It's my fault," I said, placing the fondant on the clean island.

Jett sloshed the caramel around in the pan and studied it. "I probably would have burned it anyway. I'll start over." His phone began playing music. "I'll be right back." He walked into the living room.

"I'm not a fan of fondant," I said, trying to roll it out. A hole ripped in the middle of it. "This is supposed to be the easy way to do it." I used my fingers to fix the holes.

"Fondant is something that gets easier as you practice," my mom said. "Once you're used to it, you know what it should feel like and how to work with it."

"I shouldn't have done it for the first time when it was for someone."

"I'm ready to lie around watching movies," Boyd said. "All this prep has me tired."

I smiled at him. "You mean that the entire two minutes you were stirring were too much for you?"

"Yep." He rubbed his arm. "I might have damaged my tennis elbow."

I turned to look at him. "You played tennis?"

He chuckled. "Nah. I'm joking."

I went back to rolling. "We should probably have a back-up in case this doesn't turn out. I doubt it will be pretty."

After what felt like forever, I got the fondant rolled out and placed on the round cake. It didn't look professional, but it wasn't bad. There were a few weird wrinkles where they shouldn't be, but the fondant flowers my mom made the day before would cover that.

Jett came into the kitchen and put the caramel pan in the sink. "That was Detective Madson."

I stopped what I was doing. "What did he say?"

"Lillith confessed to putting something in Wayne's drink when they searched her house and found some suspicious stuff. She claims she was only trying to scare him into leaving her alone."

"Does he believe her?"

"He's not sure what to think. Wayne's car is gone. Detective Madson thinks Lillith might have gone to his house. If he was drugged and not unconscious, she might have been able to get him into the car and somehow disposed of him."

"What did she have to say?"

"She said she didn't see him after the party, but that she tried to go over to make sure he was alright, but he didn't answer the door. She said she doesn't know how the shoe got into Frank's garden."

"Who buries a shoe? Could Frank have lied and buried it? Maybe he thought it would somehow point to Lillith?"

"Possibly. He was digging back there."

"What if Lillith drugged him, but Frank finished him off?"

"The police are looking into that possibility. It would be better if they could find a body. Without one, there isn't a lot of evidence."

"What about the blood? That wouldn't happen from poison."

"They don't have an explanation for that."

I blew out a frustrated breath. "This isn't going to be solved before we have to leave."

"Probably not. Detective Madson said he'll keep me informed."

Boyd leaned against the counter and crossed his arms. "Lillith looks like a criminal. She probably did it."

Jett grinned. "You can't tell who's guilty by how they look."

"I guess not."

"What will happen to Ginger?" I asked.

Jett shrugged.

"I bet she's hungry. Boyd should go feed her."

"Let me call Detective Madson again and see if we can take the snake until everything is figured out."

A rapid knock sounded on the door, and before my mom could get to it, Chelsea came flying down the hall. She used to do that when we were little.

"Chelsea, why don't you come in?" my mom said.

"Sorry, Candy," she said, then she looked at Jett. "Someone was looking in my window last night. I told the police, but they think I'm making it up so my mom doesn't look as guilty. I'm not. Someone was there."

"You saw them? Jett asked.

"Yes. It was a quick flash, and then they were gone."

"Did you tell Frank?"

"Yes. He thinks I'm imagining things because I was alone in the house at night."

"Did you see any of their features?" I asked.

"No. It was so fast, but I know I wasn't imagining it."

"Could it have been an animal?"

"No, but speaking of animals, I saw your cat outside. He's by the porch."

I frowned. Creepers rarely went outside without being bribed. "I'll be back."

I went out, and sure enough, Creepers was in my mom's flower bed. "What do you think you're doing?" He meowed and ran to the sidewalk. He was chasing something I couldn't see. Probably a bug. He pounced. I scooped him up and ran my hand over his gray head. "I don't want you getting lost."

I glanced over at Wayne's house and saw something move in the upstairs window.

"Great," I muttered. I rushed back inside and to the kitchen. "Someone is in Wayne's house."

Jett frowned. "It's probably the police."

I put Creepers on the floor. "There aren't any cars."

"They might have parked down the road so as not to draw attention."

"So it might be someone else." I didn't add that it could be Frank. Not in front of Chelsea.

Chelsea tugged on her long braid and frowned. "I might go on vacation or something until this is all over. It's getting scary."

"I wouldn't suggest that," Jett said. "Not until things are settled. The police will pay more attention to you if you leave because it makes it look like you're hiding something."

She bit her lip. "I guess. Frank said I could stay with him. Maybe I'll do that."

Jett was watching me.

"What?" I asked.

"I'm going to knock on Wayne's door and see what happens. If I don't, I'm sure you'll be in there, searching."

"I'll go with you."

He nodded, and we went to Wayne's. It wasn't surprising when no one answered. A car pulled up, and Detective Madson and his partner got out.

"What's going on?" he asked as they walked up the sidewalk.

"I saw someone upstairs in the window," I told him.

He frowned. "We'll go check."

"Someone needs to feed his snake."

He cringed. "If no one is there, you can take the snake until I decide what to do with it."

I nodded. They went inside.

"You want to take care of a snake?" Jett asked me as we waited. "You know what they eat, right?"

"I don't really want to, but someone has to take care of her. Boyd knows how to feed them."

"Okay."

Someone yelled from inside. I looked at Jett.

"Go back home," he commanded.

"Never."

The door burst open, and a figure in a black mask came tearing from the house. He wasn't expecting us to be there and slammed into Jett, knocking them both from the porch. They landed on the sidewalk, and Jett wrestled him to his back.

Detective Madson and his partner came rushing out. Detective Madson had a bloody lip.

Jett had the man pinned to the ground. Madson pulled the mask off, and an unfamiliar man's face appeared. He had curly brown hair and a goatee. I put him at about fifty.

Detective Madson wiped blood on his sleeve. His partner had a gun pointed at the man.

"Who are you?" Detective Madson asked.

The man was breathing hard. "I didn't do anything."

"Breaking and entry? Assaulting an officer?"

"You scared me. This is my cousin's house."

"So you're here, wearing all black and a mask, and you weren't doing anything suspicious?"

"I didn't want people to wonder who I was."

"And you thought wearing a mask was the way to do that?"

"Get this guy off me."

"Will you be good?" Jett asked.

"Yes."

Jett stood and so did the man. He brushed off his pants.

"I was only checking on my cousin's house. My mom told me he was missing. I have a key for situations like this."

Detective Madson glared at him. "Empty your pockets."

"Excuse me?"

"You heard. Don't make this harder than it has to be."

He pulled out a wad of cash, a watch, and a cell phone. "It's all mine."

I raised my eyebrow. I'd snooped through the house. I knew all that stuff was in the nightstand by Wayne's bed.

"No," said the detective. "That was all in the house." He pulled out his handcuffs and turned to me. "I'm taking this man in. Go ahead and take the snake."

I nodded, and Jett and I entered the house.

"I didn't think Wayne had any family," I said. "What if that man was the one doing weird things like feeding the snake and putting expired things in the house. That still seems so strange."

Unless someone wanted the house to feel *lived in.* But why? Was it guilt? Or was this something else entirely?

Jett nodded. "What if he killed Wayne, and it wasn't Lillith?"

"I wonder." We went into Wayne's room. Ginger was hiding under a fake rock. "Can you carry the tank? It's big."

"Yep."

"Her water's full," I said, frowning. "And that's fresh lettuce in there. Someone's been here."

Jett glanced toward the window. "Who's feeding her if no one's living here?"

"Snakes don't eat lettuce..."

I unplugged the light and the heat source. My mom wasn't going to be happy about a snake in the house. Even a pink one.

Chapter 15

"This is *A Christmas Carol*?" Jett asked, shoving a handful of popcorn into his mouth. "Where's Kermit?"

Boyd laughed. "Kids these days."

My dad turned up the volume. "We can watch that version next."

I cuddled up to Jett and tried to focus on the movie and not the man in Wayne's house. I wondered if he was the one who ruined Jett's truck and graffitied the diner.

"Wait!" my mom said. "Pause the show."

My dad paused it and shot her a questioning look.

"We forgot about Christmas pajamas. We can't watch the show without them." She rushed from the room, and my dad and I groaned. My mom got the worst matching

Christmas pajamas for us every year. I secretly loved them, but I didn't want to wear them in front of anyone.

She came back out with a stack of packages and handed one to everyone. I opened mine and sighed with relief. Red-and-black plaid. That was less embarrassing than an obscure cartoon.

"Everyone go change and be back in five," she commanded.

I hurried and put mine on and beat everyone else back to the couch. Jett came next and sat next to me. I smirked.

"What?" he asked, putting his arm over my shoulders.

"You remind me of a commercial."

He looked down at the plaid material. "Well, you match me."

"We're like one big family," Boyd said, coming in and sitting down. "I haven't had a Christmas Eve this fun in years."

"Well, you should come every year," my mom said, bringing Creepers into the room and holding him up. "Look at this!" Creepers was wearing pajamas that matched ours. He meowed in protest, and my mom put him on the floor. He ran over and jumped on my lap.

"I don't think he's a fan," I said. He stared at me, probably trying to beg me to take the pajamas off.

"Let him get used to it."

My dad was last. He sat down and grabbed the remote and started the movie. Boyd fell asleep during the first movie. My parents made it through half of the second.

"Your parents have every Christmas decoration," Jett said quietly near my ear. "Why don't they have mistletoe?"

I kissed his chin. "Do we still need it?"

"Just kiss her," my dad mumbled. "We aren't paying attention."

Jett grinned. "I like your dad."

Christmas morning came early, with Boyd knocking on my door. "Santa came! Why are you still sleeping?"

I turned over and looked at the clock. Five. I guessed when you fell asleep at six like Boyd kept doing, five wasn't so early. I rolled out of bed and stretched. Creepers crawled up from his spot at my feet to my pillow and curled up.

"You're going to miss Christmas," I told him. He glared at me, then closed his eyes.

"Are you coming?" Boyd asked, pounding on the door.

"I'm coming."

"I'll give you five minutes."

I hurried to the bathroom and ran a brush through my hair and brushed my teeth. I wouldn't do that if Jett weren't here. He'd seen me look much worse, but I still try.

I was the last one downstairs. My mom was kneeling by the tree, and the others were all sitting. Jett looked like he could use a few more hours of sleep. Boyd was the only person who looked fully awake and ready to go. I sat next to Jett. My mom liked to open presents one at a time. She passed them out, and everyone had to open them while being stared at by the others.

I didn't usually mind this tradition, but it was more awkward having people here besides family. Boyd was enthused the entire time. Every present he opened got him more excited than I'd ever seen him. I felt bad that he'd spent so many Christmases alone. I would make sure he always had a place for holidays.

After presents, I sat staring at the fireplace with Jett. Boyd was helping my mom in the kitchen, and my dad had gone back to bed. I was wearing the new boots my parents gave me. Boyd had teased me about my fashion choice since I was still wearing my plaid pajamas.

"What are you thinking?" Jett asked.

"Not much. My brain is humming."

"I thought you might be thinking of staying here until everything was solved."

I shook my head. "I need to get back. There might be clues back in Muddy Creek. I keep thinking Wayne's cousin has to be the one who messed with things."

"Why, though? If Lillith killed Wayne, that wouldn't affect the cousin. His name's Danny, by the way. Detective Madson texted me last night.

"What if Danny killed him?" I said. "He might have gone to Wayne's house that night and realized there was something off because of whatever Lillith gave him. Since they're cousins, it might not have been hard to get him into the car and drive him off somewhere. Then he waits a while and goes to steal things from his house."

"Could be."

"The buried shoe is still the weirdest thing."

"It is weird. Especially since Frank was digging there just before. That makes me wonder about Frank. What if he knew Lillith had done something, and he was trying to hide the evidence?"

"But why would a shoe be evidence?"

"I'm not sure. How's the snake?"

"I haven't checked today. It's nice of my dad to take care of her. I know my mom isn't thrilled." My dad put Wayne's pet in his office in the basement. My mom never went in there. I would bet my dad was hoping she would forget about Ginger, and he could finally have a pet.

While we were eating breakfast, someone came to the door.

"I've got it," I said, popping up. I opened the door to see Frank standing there with a box. My dad was right behind me.

"Merry Christmas," Frank said. "Do you have a minute?"

I looked back at my dad. He stepped forward. "Morning, Frank. What can we do for you?"

"One of my decorations was falling off my house. I grabbed a ladder and climbed up. I found a camera hidden under the eaves."

My dad rubbed his chin. "That's odd."

"And that's not all." He tipped the box so we could see inside. It was full of cameras. "I found all of these attached to my house and Lillith's. I can see one above your porch. They're pretty well hidden."

My dad stepped out on the porch, and Frank pointed something out to him.

"This had to be recent," my dad said. "At least after all the decorating."

"I'll help you look for more if you want," Frank offered.

My dad looked at me. "Go finish breakfast." He pulled the door closed. Normally, I would ignore him and go out, but I was hungry and tired, and he would tell me what they found.

I went back to my breakfast and told the others what happened.

My mom tapped her finger on the table. "I saw a man with a ladder doing something on Lillith's house about a week ago. I didn't think anything of it. She always hires

160

help to do things, so it isn't odd to see a stranger doing something."

"Do you remember what he looked like?" I asked, taking a bite of bacon.

"Not at all."

Jett put his fork down. "Did they call Detective Madson?"

"I'm not sure."

"That's what they should do first." He stood and pushed in his chair. "We should probably check Wayne's house as well. I'm going to go out and talk to them." He grabbed his plate and put it in the sink, then left.

My mom sighed. "This is all getting out of hand. Should we be nervous? What's the point of the cameras?"

"It's hard to know. How could someone do all that without being seen?"

"It's like I said. I saw someone and didn't think about it. All the neighbors would be the same. Everyone would figure it was someone putting up decorations or fixing something."

"Did they announce the winner of the Christmas decorations?"

My mom gave a small smile. "Yep. Last night. The winner was someone around the corner. Dad came in second and Frank third."

"Could the cameras be someone who really wanted to win?" Boyd asked.

I moved my lips from side to side. "I think it's more likely connected to Wayne, but anything's possible. Lilith wasn't even in the competition. Maybe Wayne being scared of cameras wasn't as unreasonable as I thought. Maybe he knew something was going on."

I impatiently helped with the dishes as we waited for my dad and Jett to come back in. Detective Madson had shown up a few minutes ago, so I would have to wait longer. By the time they came in, I was going crazy.

"There were three cameras on the house and three on Wayne's," Jett told me. "All battery-powered. Someone rigged them with motion sensors so they'd only record when someone moved nearby. There was also one in Wayne's house in his room. It was hidden pretty well. Detective Madson is having a team come to search more thoroughly."

A camera in the bedroom? Either Wayne was watching someone—or someone was watching him.

"Do you think they were just watching, or recording something?" I asked.

"Hard to say," Jett said. "Depends on who set them up—and why."

My mom put a hand to her heart. "Does that mean there might be cameras in here?"

Jett looked around the kitchen. "I doubt it, but I can check closely to make sure."

"Thanks, Jett," she said, walking over and kissing his cheek. He was going to have to get used to that.

"I'll help," I said, taking his hand. "Where was the camera at Wayne's?"

"It was in a black picture frame. It was easy to spot once you knew it was there, but it blended in well. I don't think anything will be here because there are usually people around. It would be easier to install cameras at Wayne's since he worked a lot."

We spent over an hour looking around the house, but nothing was out of the ordinary. At noon, I realized I was still in my pajamas. I went and showered and got dressed, then I paced across my room. Anything we were going to find had to be today.

The cousin weighed on my mind. If Danny was family, why hadn't anyone heard of him before? Why now, just when Wayne was gone and everything felt upside down?

Creepers couldn't figure out what I was doing. He batted at my pants every time I passed him.

The door opened, and Jett poked his head in. "Is this what we're doing for the rest of the day?"

"What do you want to do?" I asked, picking up Creepers.

"I don't know. Boyd wants to play chess, and that's definitely not what I want to do."

"I want to figure out what happened with Wayne, but I don't have any ideas. I don't know what to check or what to do."

"It's not always possible to solve everything. I had to accept that a few years ago."

I nodded, but I couldn't let it go. Something about it all didn't add up. No body, nothing helpful. Just a missing man and a house full of strange details.

"What do you think of my new shirt?" he asked, holding out his arms to show off his green shirt.

I smiled. "I think whoever got that for you has great taste." I went over and put my hands behind his neck.

"Excellent taste," he said, putting his hands on my waist.

I stress a lot about presents. I'd gotten Jett a few presents, hoping he would like at least one of them.

"Who's up for chess?" Boyd asked, coming in.

Jett groaned. "Boyd, can't you read a room?"

Boyd chuckled. "I don't try to. That makes life too complicated."

"Go ask my dad," I suggested. "He likes chess."

"Alright." He disappeared from the room.

"I love Boyd," Jett said, "but he is never living with us."

I laughed. "Noted."

"I'm not joking. I know you, Ivs."

I kissed him softly. "What if we build a house? We could put in an in-law apartment. Then he would have his own place, but be close."

"Nope. Still too close. His condo will be built soon. That's not far from the diner. He can walk there in a minute."

"True."

"He's still in fairly good health. You don't have to worry about him."

"Did you see how happy he was this morning? I don't want him to be alone on holidays."

"He's never alone. Most years, he does things with Barbra, Opal, and their little group. I'm fine with him coming over for holidays if he wants to. I just don't want him popping in every time I try to kiss you."

"Who are we talking about?" Boyd asked, poking his head in. "I can't find your dad."

Jett released me. "I give up. Let's go find Hank."

Chapter 16

"She's back!" Livy exclaimed when I walked into the diner the following afternoon.

José poked his head out the serving window. "Welcome back! Did you have a good Christmas?"

"Yes, how about you?" I asked. "It was your first Christmas with Carrie."

"It was great. A lot more fun than being alone. How was the flight?"

"Good. Creepers isn't a fan of flying."

"Where is he?"

"Boyd's taking him upstairs to calm him down. I bet I'll never get him in a carrier again."

I glanced around the diner. There wasn't a single patron.

"The day after holidays is always a little dead."

"José painted the back of the diner," Livy said, pulling on her red ponytail. "You can't tell anything happened."

"Thanks," I told him.

"Not a problem. Christmas Eve was slow and not snowy, so I took care of it. Carrie helped."

"Is she here?"

"Nope. Just me and Livy. I knew it would be slow, so I didn't want you paying a bunch of people to stand around. Did you solve the case?"

My shoulders slumped. "No. Jett thinks the police will figure it out. We did find out who drugged him. I still think she might have killed him, but he also has a cousin who was stealing from his house. It's hard to know. Maybe if I'd had more time. Can I see the video of the person who did the graffiti?"

"Sure. I put it on my phone. I was going to send it to you, but I figured you were busy enough." He came out of the kitchen with his phone and pulled something up. "It's only a small piece."

I watched a man spray-paint on the diner. With a ski mask, it was impossible to tell who it might be. "I'm guessing there isn't a lot of difference between black masks, but that looks just like Wayne's cousin did when he was caught stealing. He's the same build as well."

"It stinks about Jett's truck."

"Yeah. Has Ledford come up with any leads?"

"Not that he's shared with me."

Livy smiled. "Did your mom get you to set a wedding date? José said he bet she would press it."

"No. I'll pick one soon. Dang. I just had a thought. I can't get married until I get Deputy Ledford and Jane to fall for each other."

Livy giggled. "You would wish Ledford on someone?"

I smiled. "He's not as bad as he wants us to think. Jett and I made a bet about Ledford and Jane. If I lose, I have to clean up after all the animals the first year we're married."

Livy's eyes glittered with excitement. "I would love to watch you try. Jane's never going to fall for him."

"You never know. I just need them to go on one date."

"Oh. That's not as bad as actually falling for each other. I bet you could get Jane to do it just so you wouldn't lose."

"No. I can't set them up or tell them."

José shook his head. "I don't think they have enough personality between them to date."

"Jane's awesome," I protested.

"Yeah, but what would they do for fun? Neither one of them strikes me as fun."

"Maybe not. I regret it now. It sounded like a good idea when we made the bet."

"Don't put your wedding off for a bet," José said. "I'm guessing Jett would call the bet off if he knew you might be dragging your feet because of it."

"I'm not going to drag my feet. I'd rather be married to Jett and be cleaning out the litter box, than not."

I sat at the table at Jett's house the next day and smiled as I watched him move around the kitchen. He'd insisted on making me dinner. He pulled some rolls from the oven, then stirred something on the stove. We were going to celebrate Christmas with his parents later today.

"Sorry it's not fancy. I can't do homemade. Did you know you can buy frozen rolls and leave them out for a while, then cook them?"

"You don't say?" I teased.

"I've learned a lot of shortcuts living on my own." He ladled something into bowls and brought them to the table. He placed one in front of me and one across the table for him, then went back to the pan of rolls.

The mixture in my bowl gave me pause. The yellow soup didn't look like it had anything in it, except maybe a few pieces of chicken. I took my spoon and stirred it around.

"Is this cream of chicken soup?"

"Yep. I've never eaten it, but I know you like soup and chicken. I had hoped it would have more chicken."

I covered my smile with my hand. I'd never eaten straight cream of chicken soup. It might be hard to get through, but I'd try it for Jett.

He brought over the steaming rolls and placed them in the middle of the table, then sat down.

I took a bite or more like a slurp of soup. He took a large spoonful and frowned. We ate silently for a few minutes. I grabbed a roll and wondered if it would be bad manners to dip my roll in the soup. My throat felt a little funny.

"This isn't very good," he said. "Sorry."

I smiled. "Most people use cream of chicken soup to cook with. I've never known anyone to eat it like soup."

He wrinkled his nose. "Then why is it called soup? You should have told me. You don't have to eat it."

I laughed. "The rolls are good."

"And I made dessert. By made, I mean I paid José to make something he doesn't usually make at the diner."

"Nice."

We ate a few more rolls, then he brought out a big glass container of chocolate mousse.

"Fancy," I said, as he scooped it into a glass. It tasted great, which wasn't surprising. José doesn't make anything that isn't good.

"I have to work tomorrow. I wish I had a few more days."

"What will you do about the truck?"

"It was insured. I'll go with a regular police truck this time."

"Not a Cybertruck?"

"Not this time. It was fun for a while, but after that wore off, it felt a little silly. I miss my old black truck. It could haul a lot. Are you working at the diner tomorrow?"

"Yes. And teaching Zumba in the morning."

Conan ran into the room, barking. He stared at me and wagged his tail.

"He's happy to be home," Jett said. "He was so excited to see Boyd yesterday. I worried he would pass out."

I got down on my knees and scratched behind Conan's ears. He put one paw on my knee and licked my hand.

"Gross. I'll never get used to the licking thing. Cats don't do that. At least Creepers doesn't."

"He bites the back of my leg when he wants attention, though. That's more annoying."

"He doesn't do it hard."

"Hard enough to make me jump every time."

I picked Conan up and cuddled him. "I hope my dad is really okay with Ginger. I think he'll love having her, but he's never had a pet. The fun might wear off after he has to clean the enclosure. My dad's never been great at cleaning up gross things. My mom said he only changed a handful of diapers because it made him gag."

Jett laughed. "Your dad seems tough."

"Nope. If anyone puked, he would go hide in his office until they were better."

"And your mom let him?"

"Yeah. She said she would rather change all the diapers and clean up puke and have him do the dishes. He's always been in charge of dishes and mopping."

"So if I say changing diapers makes me gag—"

I tilted my head. "Don't even think about it. You're changing diapers. Your job is gross sometimes. I'm pretty sure you can handle a diaper."

He chuckled. "Yeah, I can handle a diaper. Probably. I've never been tested."

"You've never changed a diaper?"

"I'm an only child. I have one cousin my age, and the rest are all much older than me. You're an only child. Have you changed a diaper?"

"I've babysat, so yes. Not a lot, though."

"Our poor kids."

I shrugged. "You can learn anything on the internet."

He laughed. "I guess that's right."

"I feel bad you weren't home for Christmas with your parents."

"They just got back from their cruise, remember? My parents aren't big on celebrations, so they didn't mind putting it off for a few days. My mom has been using the same Christmas tree decorations for as long as I can remember. The only ones that changed were the ones I made at school. It's a pretty sad-looking tree."

Conan squirmed, so I put him down. I hope the Malones liked my gifts. They would pretend to, whether they did or not. I'd gotten them the same things I got my parents because I didn't know what they liked.

That evening, when we arrived at the Malones' house, his mom, Carol, met us at the door. "Come in, come in!" She hugged me. "Did you have a good Christmas?"

"It was nice."

"Wonderful. Come this way."

Jett took off his jacket. "Am I invited?"

Carol patted his shoulder. "Hello, Jett. It's good to see you." She turned and linked arms with me. "I hope you're ready for a stomachache. We have donuts and chocolate milk. That's probably the only tradition we do every year. Jett's probably grown out of it, but I can't let it go."

"I'll never grow out of donuts," Jett said from behind us.

Jett's dad was in the living room setting up a game of Catan.

"Games might be tradition as well. Watch out. Jett and Tanner both cheat."

"Hi, Tanner," I said.

Jett's dad turned and smiled. "It's good to have you, Ivy."

"Do you need help?" Jett asked, bending over the card table.

"I've almost got it," Tanner said. "I'm a little jet-lagged from flying back from the cruise, but I have a few good hours in me."

"I'll bring in the donuts and chocolate milk," Carol said.

"Do you need help?" I asked.

"That would be nice." I followed her to the kitchen, and she pointed at a brown box. "If you wanna grab that, I'll get the milk and cups."

I took the donuts into the living room and handed them to Jett. There was a second card table that Jett put them on.

Carol brought the chocolate milk and cups and put them on the table next to the donuts. "Go ahead and help yourself. We don't judge here. Jett drinks so much chocolate milk every year he gets sick."

Jett tilted his head. "Come on, Ma. I haven't done that in years. I have better control now."

It was a lie. An hour later, Jett was lying on the couch, holding his stomach.

"What did I say?" Carol asked.

I smiled and helped Tanner clean off the table. I was just glad the game was over. I'd never played with people who were so brutal. They would cut someone off even if it wasn't their best move, just to annoy each other.

Jett's phone vibrated, and he looked at the screen. "It's Detective Madson. I'll be back." He groaned and held his stomach as he left the room.

I forced myself to stay where I was. With luck, the detective had solved the case, and I wouldn't have to think about it every minute.

Jett came back and sat on the couch, leaning forward, his elbows resting on his legs. He looked at me with a serious expression.

"A body turned up at the sewer plant."

I swallowed. "Wayne's?"

He shook his head. "They haven't identified the body yet, but Detective Madson said the man wasn't heavy like Wayne."

"Then why did he call you?"

"He thinks it's connected. He believes he knows who it is, but he doesn't want to say without knowing for sure."

"Why?"

"He doesn't want to spread rumors that aren't true."

My phone buzzed. I looked at it. It was Chelsea. She hadn't called me in years.

"Hello?"

"Ivy?" Chelsea's voice trembled. "It's Wayne's cousin. They just found his body at the sewer plant."

I sat straighter. "What?"

"It's all over town. Ivy... someone killed him."

Chapter 17

My mind couldn't concentrate on Zumba the following morning. I went through the motions, and I kept a smile on my face, but my mind was in Arizona. Who would have killed Danny? Why wasn't he locked away for being in Wayne's house stealing things?

Of course, Chelsea was only saying what Frank guessed from talking to the police. Danny might not be the one who died, but that was what Frank took away. I danced around, not even feeling amused by the crazy moves from my students.

I threw my hands in the air and watched my class copy me. Some of them had improved a lot since they started. It made me feel like I was positively contributing to the community. I had students tell me they were moving better than they had in years. It was amazing what a little exercise could do.

Wayne's shoe was going to haunt me for eternity. I needed to know why it was in Frank's garden. I thought of the dirty shoe in the closet. Wayne was such a neat freak, so I was surprised he had a dirty shoe. It wouldn't be shocking to learn he washed his shoes weekly.

I stopped, and my smile slipped. When I first went to Wayne's house after he disappeared, his bed was messy. I'd noticed because he was so neat. Later, the bed had been made. The police wouldn't make his bed.

How had I missed it? The bed. The shoe. The spotless fridge with mold. Wayne wasn't dead. He was playing a game.

And I'd been dancing around like a fool while he watched it unfold.

"What's wrong, deary?" Barbra asked.

"Wayne's messing with me," I muttered. "He's not dead."

My class all stared blankly at me. I could almost hear them blinking.

"Who's Wayne?" Opal asked.

"I have to go," I said, rushing to my coat and bag. I pulled my coat on and hurried out the door. The freezing snow blew into my face, but I ignored it and went to the sheriff's office. By the time I got there, my shoes were soaked through.

I walked through the doors, and Jane smiled at me. "Hi, Ivy. Looking for Sheriff Malone?"

"Yes. Is he here?"

"Ivs?" Jett said, coming out of his office.

"Wayne isn't dead."

"How do you know?"

"I don't for sure, but I feel it. He's messing with me."

"Why would he do that?"

"He's obsessed with what I do. I'm not sure of his motive. He might be trying to outsmart me. When we went into his house, his bed wasn't made. When we went back, it was. Who would sneak into a person's house and make their bed?"

"The same person who snuck in and put rotten mayo in his fridge?"

"I bet he planted that, just to confuse me. This entire ordeal has to be some crazy thing he's made up in his head. What if he buried that shoe just to throw me off?"

"I guess he could have. But where is he?"

I chewed the inside of my cheek and thought. "He told me he has a vacation house."

"The guy in the video wasn't Wayne. There's no way."

"I bet it was Danny. He was some kind of accomplice. We need to go to Arizona."

Jett's mouth turned down. "I can't take any more time off this month. Just call Detective Madson and tell him your suspicion." He rubbed a spot on his shoulder.

"Is something wrong? You've been rubbing your shoulder for a few days."

He grimaced. "When Danny plowed into me and we fell off the porch, I hit hard. It's not terrible, just annoying."

I nodded. "Take it easy and let it get better. I'll see you." I hurried out of the building and went to the library. If I called Detective Madson, he would think I was crazier than he already did. I went in and frowned. A woman I didn't know sat behind the desk.

"Can I help you?" she asked.

"Is Brian here?"

"No. Mr. Cooper is out of town."

"Right," I muttered. I braved the snow one more time and jogged home. I went into my apartment and tossed my wet shoes. Creepers moseyed over and sniffed one of them. I sank onto the couch and dialed Brian.

"Hello?" he answered.

"Hi. Is there a way you can figure out where a property someone owns is?"

"I'm great. How are you?" he teased.

"Sorry. How are you?"

He laughed. "It's fine. I'm sure you're in the middle of something. I can probably find it out for you."

"It's tough when you aren't at the library."

"It won't be forever. It might be longer than I first thought, though. Tell me the information you know, and I'll try to figure it out for you."

"Thanks." I told him what I knew about Wayne and hung up. There wasn't anything else I could do, so I went downstairs to help in the diner.

There were more people than the day before, but it was far from crowded. I went into the kitchen to find Anton and José working hard.

"Do you need help?" I asked.

José looked over his shoulder. "Can you butter the rolls? There's some melted butter in the microwave."

"Sure." I grabbed the melted butter and spread it across the rolls. Now that I had a theory, it would be a struggle for me not to act. Not that there was anything I could do.

"What's wrong?" Anton asked. "You're glaring at the rolls."

"You don't want to know," I said.

"Probably not."

"There's a guy we thought got killed in Arizona, but I think he faked it."

Anton groaned. "How does this stuff find you?"

"I don't know. Brian's looking up some information for me. Waiting isn't my thing."

"Don't do anything dangerous," José warned.

My phone rang. "Brian?"

"It was easy to find. Wayne owns a small cabin near a lake. Do you have a pencil? I have the address."

I looked around and grabbed one of the server's notepads and pencils. Brian gave me the address. I was going back to Arizona.

"You aren't taking off, are you?" José asked.

"Maybe."

"To Arizona?"

"Yes."

"Does Jett know?"

"Nope. He'd stop me."

José pulled off his apron. "Let me call Carrie and have her come over. I'm coming with you."

I thought of protesting, but I wanted him to come, and he probably knew that. I might occasionally jump into things without a great plan, but I do like to have a friend at my side.

"Anton?" I said.

"I'm not coming."

I smiled. "I need you to tell Jett. But not until I've had time to get on the plane. Also, tell Boyd to watch Creepers."

"That I can handle."

I grabbed my phone and turned off my location. If Jett saw me on my way to Wichita, he would be suspicious. I hoped there was a flight.

Creepers didn't care I was going. I told him goodbye and tried to give him a kiss, but he batted at me. I was only taking a small carry-on. I'd called and booked two seats on a plane that would leave in three hours. We needed to hustle.

José drove us to Wichita, and we made it onto the plane without trouble. I sat back and sighed. My phone rang. It was Jett. I ignored it. If I answered, he could talk me out of going.

"He's going to be annoyed," José said.

"Probably. He shouldn't know yet unless Anton panicked and told him."

The phone beeped, and I listened to Jett's message. "Pick up, Ivs. I can't track you. That means either one, you're in trouble, or two, you're on your way to Arizona."

"You can't let him worry," José said.

I nodded and sent him a text. *I'm fine. I have to turn off my phone. Go talk to Anton. Talk to you later.* As soon as it sent, I turned off the phone.

"There. He knows I'm safe."

"You should have told him you were with me. He'd feel a little better knowing you aren't alone."

"If he talks to Anton, he'll know."

"How's Brian? It's strange to go into the library and not see him."

"I think he's good."

"Do you know what he's doing? He was vague about it."

"He's helping a woman in Nebraska start a library."

"That'll be good for him. He never leaves the library here. He could use a change of scenery."

I smiled. "By going to another library?"

"Meeting new people will be good."

"He's excited about it. I'm surprised Carrie let you go off without any hesitation."

"We both lived on our own long enough, so we aren't bothered by a little solitude. I assume this is a fast trip?"

"I hope so."

⁂

We rented a car at the airport and drove for a few hours across Arizona.

"It's nice to leave the snow behind," José said. "I like a little snow, but after Christmas, I'm ready for spring."

I nodded and looked out at the desert as it passed by. "I've only had two snowy winters, and I'm ready to move to Hawaii."

"I only want snow if I don't have to go anywhere."

"Me too. I do like to watch it when I'm staying in. My bedroom window has a great view."

"What do we do when we get to this place? There's a good chance there might be a crazy guy inside."

"I have pepper spray."

"That's not reassuring."

"Wayne's a big guy. Not in the muscly way. He doesn't move fast."

José turned off the highway and onto a two-lane road. "You should call Jett."

"I will. Later."

"How many times has he called?"

"Only three. He's texted a bunch more."

José sighed. "You and Jett are getting married. You don't want to do things that might damage your relationship."

I laughed. "What are you talking about?"

"When you run off and do things like this, it stresses Jett. I know you're doing what you think is best, but you also need to respect Jett's feelings. You need to make compromises and care about what he's thinking."

"I do care."

"But you let your passions guide you. Sometimes you need to stop and think about how your actions affect him."

I frowned and stared at the passing cacti.

"What if Jett took off and didn't tell you what he was doing, but you knew he was in danger?"

My frown deepened. I would hate that. I already had to block out knowing he could be in danger at his job every day. If he left and wouldn't answer his phone, I would be livid.

I pulled out my phone and stared at it. I didn't want to call and have a conversation in front of José. If I called him, I might cry, and I definitely didn't want José to see that. I settled on a text.

I'm sorry I took off and didn't answer the phone. That was rude of me. I'm with José. I love you. I'll try to do better. I can't talk on the phone right now.

I stared at the screen. If he left and wouldn't answer *me*, I'd lose my mind.

I didn't want to lose him over this.

Not over Wayne.

He texted back. *I love you. Please share your location with me again.*

I fiddled with my phone so he could see where I was. Now I was going to sit here and try not to feel guilty for the rest of the ride.

José slowed the car. "That's the turn."

I stared down the narrow dirt road, my stomach twisting.

If Wayne was waiting for us, that could be bad. If he wasn't, I needed a new plan.

Chapter 18

This was it. I stood with José in front of a white cottage-style house near a lake. Either Wayne was inside or my hunch was completely wrong. If it was wrong, I wasn't sure what the next move should be.

And if I was wrong, if this whole thing was some fever dream cooked up from a messy bed and a lost shoe, I'd flown across the country chasing a ghost.

Worse, I'd dragged someone I cared about into it.

"Do we knock or go peek in windows?" I wondered. The curtains were all open.

"I'm not sure," José said. "I'm surprised the police didn't come here."

"They think he's dead. If someone took him from his house, they wouldn't take him to his own vacation spot."

We walked up to the door, and I tried to see in the small window at the top. It was too distorted. I started to knock, but the door slid open as soon as I touched it.

I looked at José and ignored the chill running down my back. "That was creepy." I pushed the doorbell, and we waited. No one came, so we went inside. I'd probably wasted a lot of money coming here.

"Hello?" I called. We walked through the immaculate house. There wasn't anything out of place. If I didn't know it was Wayne's, I would think no one had ever been in here.

I opened a door and sucked in a breath. Wayne sat at a computer. He swiveled the chair around and smiled at me.

"I've never been so happy to see a person in my life," he said.

My eyes narrowed. "What do you think you're doing?"

"Are you going to introduce me to José?" he asked. "I'm glad he gets to be involved. I was sad when he didn't come for Christmas."

I glanced at José, then back. "We aren't here for that."

"Okay. What do you think I'm doing?"

"I think you set up an elaborate scheme because you are pathetically obsessed with me."

"Ivy..." José warned.

Wayne's smile cracked. "That's not fair."

I raised my eyebrows.

He straightened and let out a shaky breath. "Okay. Maybe it is. But obsession is just admiration taken seriously."

"What?"

Wayne shrugged. "It's true. I wanted to be part of the Ivy Clark experience. I couldn't think of a way to do it. Then at your parents' party, I saw Lillith put something in my eggnog. The idea popped into my head, and I have to say, it's been brilliant. The last few days were a bummer because my cameras all got taken down, and I thought you gave up on me."

"You put Chelsea's earring in your house."

He ran a hand over the unruly sides of his hair. "She lost it at the party, so I grabbed it. I knew that would put you on her scent."

"And the shoe? You just buried it to be annoying?"

He laughed. "I saw Frank digging in the garden, and I saw you watching. I knew it would confuse you to no end."

"But you messed up. When you disappeared, your bed was a mess. Later, it was made."

His eyes sparkled. "And you think that was a mistake? I did that to see how sharp you are. I knew it was a risk coming back to do those things, but it was worth it, and Ginger needed to be fed. I assume you're taking care of her?"

"How does Danny play into this?"

"Danny's as bribable as anyone you've ever seen. He helped install the cameras."

"Was he the one looking in Chelsea's window?"

"Probably. I asked him to keep a watch on everyone."

"And to leave threatening notes, ruin trucks, and spray-paint my diner?"

He held out his hands in surrender. "Don't blame me for that. He was only supposed to leave notes, but he got carried away."

"So you killed him?"

His brow came together. "Why would I kill him? I need him for things."

"You know you're going to be in a lot of trouble, right?"

"Only if I get caught."

José cocked his head. "You're already caught, buddy."

"Only if you turn me in. I was annoyed you got the police involved. I thought you would solve it before that happened."

"I tell the police things," I insisted.

"I figured you'd tell your boyfriend, but I didn't think you would do that here. Now I'm in a mess trying to figure out how to let people know I'm alive without getting in trouble. I would pin it on Danny, but he would rat me out."

"And he's dead," I said.

His eyes went wide. "Why do you keep saying that? I talked to him the other day."

"Well, today, he's dead. Found in the sewer plant."

"Oh, wow." He ran a hand over his face.

I put my hands on my hips. "Don't try to pretend you didn't do it."

"I didn't. Danny's my cousin. Why would I hurt him?"

"Why did you do any of this?"

"I told you. For you. I thought, what would I like more than anything in the world? To date Ivy Clark. Well, I knew that wasn't going to happen, so what was the next best thing? To have Ivy Clark solve my murder."

"What about the blood in your house?" I was trying not to think about his odd obsession, but it wasn't easy.

"That was a happy coincidence. I hurt myself by accident and decided to wipe the blood on the floor. It added something nice, I thought. I hope I can get the stain out. I did a lot of things to help you along. I left my back door unlocked. Even here, I left the door slightly ajar. That was a great touch, wasn't it?"

"You ruined my Christmas vacation because you're unhinged."

"Ruined? I made it memorable. You like solving mysteries, or you wouldn't do it. Now I guess you can solve Danny's murder."

"It was you. You planted a notebook at the sewer plant. You wrote that the screening area was ideal."

Wayne's smile slipped slightly. "That wasn't written in there."

"I saw it," I said. "You wrote that the screening area was ideal. The same spot where Danny was dumped."

"I write notes all the time," he said, his smile twitching. "Could've been anything."

"No." He stood and walked to a metal filing cabinet. He pulled out a notebook similar to the one at the plant and flipped pages.

"Did you write it in the wrong book?" I asked.

His face went pale. "That could mean anything. I work there. A lot of things about the screening area is ideal."

"Nothing I saw. How did you get Danny in there and push him without anyone seeing you? Nothing was on the cameras, but then you know about cameras. You claimed you don't like cameras, but you must."

Wayne shook his head and smiled. He clapped his hands slowly. "I salute you. I really do. It's been a privilege watching you work. I wish I could have watched from closer range."

"Why kill Danny? You obviously planned that before I came, or it wouldn't be in the notebook."

"Danny was a thief and an idiot. He was always stealing from me, and I'd had enough. I do know a lot about computers and cameras. I made a distraction at the plant and hurried Danny in. He never knew what was coming."

"And now you've admitted it."

"To you. Now I have a conundrum."

I took a few steps closer. José was right behind me.

Wayne pulled out a gun and pointed it at us. "This really is going to be difficult."

"People know we're here," I told him. "Don't be stupid."

"I'll come up with something."

"No. They already know about you. Do you really think I would come without letting people know?" I'd done it before, but now wasn't the time to bring that up. I walked closer to his desk at enough of an angle not to make him panic.

"Stop coming closer."

I stood next to the desk and turned to him. "Something else will take you down."

"What?" he asked.

"Why should I tell you?"

"Because it might save you. I don't want to hurt you, but you're pushing the boundaries."

"It's your computer." I motioned to the thin desktop screen.

He swallowed, and the gun lowered slightly. "Nothing on there is incriminating."

"Look," I said, pointing at it. "It's not what's inside." He bent down, and his eyes narrowed as he studied it.

I grabbed the screen and, in one fluid motion, slammed it into his head and shoulder. He fell to the ground and dropped the gun, and the computer crashed next to him. Before I could blink, José had the gun pointed at Wayne.

I smiled down at him. "I told you it would take you down."

He put a hand to the side of his head and didn't get up. "I should have seen that coming. I remember the story about you hitting someone with the lid to a toilet tank. You broke my computer."

"And I would do it again."

"I bet you bruised my skull." He grinned and shook his head. "At least if I have to go down, I was taken down by Ivy Clark. Not everyone can say that. Wow, I'm dizzy."

"Call the police," José said.

"Detective Madson or 911?" I asked.

"Call 911. I'm not sure whether this is the same jurisdiction, and if he's in the same city as the airport, it will take too long for him to get here."

Wayne sat up and held his head. José kept the gun focused on him. I pulled out my phone and called the police.

"They'll be here soon," I said, putting it back in my pocket.

Wayne swayed and went back to his back. "I bet you gave me a concussion. I could sue for that."

"You can't sue me for defending myself. You had a gun."

"This has all been interesting. I hope I can get it all on my *Ivy Clark Fan Page.* I wish you hadn't broken my computer. I could have downloaded some videos before the police got here."

I just looked at Wayne. I couldn't comprehend the way he thought. I tried not to look at the side of his head, but my eyes kept drifting over. He was going to have a massive bruise and bump.

It felt like the police took their time. It was probably worse for José. He had to hold the gun up the entire time. I stopped talking to Wayne. Everything he said only irritated me. Once he realized I wasn't going to respond, he stopped talking. Now he just stared up at the ceiling. He probably had a colossal headache.

Four police officers came in with their guns drawn. They didn't have any trouble cuffing Wayne. They stood him up, and he swayed. Two of the officers took him out, and the other two wanted me to tell them everything that had happened. I gave them my number and informed them that Detective Madson was leading the case.

It was time to relax. At least once we got home. I was in the mood for a pizza and a movie marathon.

Chapter 19

I sat at my parents' kitchen table, drinking hot chocolate with Chelsea. It felt strangely peaceful. No snide comments, no competition, just two tired women sharing cocoa.

I was trying to forget about yesterday. We'd driven to my parents' house, and by the time we arrived, it was late. Now I was tired, but glad things were settled.

"Do you know what's going to happen with your mom?" I asked.

"No. Her lawyer thinks she'll get fined and possibly have a small amount of jail time. I can't believe she never told me Frank was my dad. I'm more annoyed about that than anything. I mean, it was bad she tried to drug Wayne, but I don't feel so bad now he turned out to be a killer."

It was strange to hear her talk so calmly about it all, like we weren't sitting in the shadow of a murder case and a fake death.

I took a sip from my mug. "Do you think your relationship with Frank will change?"

"I'm not sure. He always treated me like a dad would anyway. He said he'd wondered a time or two if he could be my dad, but he thought that was ridiculous. I wonder if that's why he paid for my college."

"What will you do?"

She rubbed the rim of her mug with her finger and frowned. "I've been too reliant on my mom. I'm old enough to be on my own, but I've never worked a job that could support me. I'll probably stay at my mom's house until I find a better job. Frank said he could help me."

"That's nice of him."

"How long are you here?"

"I couldn't get a flight until tomorrow morning."

"I guess if I can't find a job around here, I could come to Kansas and work with you."

I hoped my smile didn't look as fake as it felt. Chelsea and I might have gotten over the past, but that didn't mean I wanted her in my diner every day.

She leaned against her chair. "Did you know Wayne stole my earring?"

"Yeah. He knew I would find it and think you were involved."

"That's so messed up. It's a good thing you're good at figuring this stuff out. I would have given up the second I saw Wayne's snake."

"Ginger is the least scary snake I've ever seen. She's pink."

Chelsea shivered. "I don't care what color they are, I don't want to be around them. It's one reason I don't do yard work."

"What are the other reasons?"

"Dirt, spiders, and sweat."

I smiled. "I see."

She stood and grabbed her phone from the table. "I need to get going. We should keep in touch. It's too bad we let our friendship slip away all those years ago. Text me anytime. And don't forget to invite me to the wedding."

I was pretty sure she didn't mean any of it, but at least we'd made it through a conversation without trying to outdo or insult each other.

"If you need any fashion help before the wedding, let me know. I can help you so you don't look like a complete wreck."

Okay. We almost made it through without insulting each other. I smiled and let her show herself out. I didn't have any more small talk left in me. I took the mugs to the sink, then went to my dad's office to check on Ginger. She was coiled up under a fake log.

I'd called Jett earlier and told him everything that had happened. He'd just sighed and said, "As long as you're safe." Which somehow made me feel worse than if he'd yelled.

The house was quiet. My dad and José were doing something out back, and my mom was at the store. She'd been thrilled to find we were stranded here for the night, and she wanted to make something special for dinner.

I wandered back up the stairs and paced around the house. I couldn't think of anything to do, and I didn't have Creepers to talk to. Now that Wayne was captured and the case was solved, I didn't have anything to contemplate. It was too bad Jett hadn't come.

I held out my left hand and stared at my diamond ring with a smile. Putting off setting a wedding date was silly. I'd lived alone long enough, and I couldn't wait to spend every day with Jett. At least the parts he wasn't working.

I sat down in the living room and called him.

"Hi, Ivs."

"Hey."

"What's going on? I hope you're at your parents' house having a dull time. I can't handle any more excitement this week."

"I'm completely bored. No one's here. I've been thinking."

"Uh-oh."

I smiled. "It's not that bad. I think we should get married."

He laughed quietly. "I thought we'd already decided that."

"How about next month?"

"In the cold, snowy weather?" he asked in mock surprise.

"I know. I can't wait to start our life together, so I can brave the cold."

"Let's do it. You pick the week."

"I love you."

"I love you too."

❧

"You put eggs on the rolls?" I asked José.

He laughed as he spread beaten egg on the raw dough. "I do it every time I make these rolls."

"I guess that's why my rolls don't taste the same. I thought you always put melted butter. And these rolls are my favorite."

"I put butter on some, but not these."

"I love rolls. That's how I choose a restaurant. By the rolls. There's a buffet in town that I love, just because of the rolls."

"I get that. Bread can be a comfort food."

My mom turned from where she was cutting potatoes. "I never liked that buffet, but that's where you always wanted to go. I didn't know you were all about the rolls."

I smiled and thought about eating rolls. "There's one restaurant that does soup, salad, and breadsticks. Sometimes I wonder what they would say if I only wanted breadsticks."

"Do you dip them in anything?" José asked.

"No. That ruins them. I dip rolls in gravy, but not my breadsticks." My mouth was watering. I hadn't eaten much for breakfast, and my body was letting me know.

After everything that had happened, this was exactly what I needed—home, food, and a little peace.

My dad came in holding a big gingerbread man under one arm. "I'm cleaning up."

"Do you need help?" I asked. "I thought you didn't like to clean up until January?"

"I usually don't. I'm just tired of it this year. It felt like too much stress. Frank is the reason I get crazy with the decorations. He told me he's thinking of moving. He's embarrassed about how everything has gone down this past week."

"Why would he be embarrassed?"

He shrugged. "I know Chelsea's been telling anyone who will listen to her that Frank's her dad. Since they don't know the story, Frank thinks it's making him look irresponsible. I doubt anyone would judge him. Most people like Frank and dislike Lillith. If he lets the real story circulate, I'm sure the majority of people would side with him."

"I actually feel bad for Chelsea."

"You shouldn't. She'll be better off with Frank in her life than she was before. He's always been involved in her life, but now I think he'll take it up a few notches."

"It's still weird to me that Lillith would lie and leave Frank just to get government help."

My mom nodded. "It's hard to understand how other people think when they're under a lot of stress. We all handle things differently, and some of us do better than others."

Chapter 20

"Isn't it time to stop the Christmas music?" Anton asked as he swept the kitchen floor in the diner. The jukebox was blaring Elvis Presley's "Blue Christmas."

"Is it still December?" I asked. "According to my calendar, it is, and that means Christmas music."

José chuckled. "Don't argue with the boss."

Anton grinned. "I wouldn't dare. I guess it's not like getting rid of the Christmas music will help. Once it stops, Boyd will be back to playing all those ancient songs that came out at the time of the dinosaurs."

I grinned and placed strawberries on a dessert. "I like those songs."

"They're even too old for you."

I raised my eyebrow. "I'm only five years older than you."

He placed the broom in the closet and pulled a hair net over his black hair. "I have to give you a hard time sometimes." He washed his hands and went to the fridge. "Couldn't we take down Christmas decorations after your party tonight?"

"Nope. January first." I was having a party at the diner tonight. One last Christmas bash before dreary January was upon us.

Livy came in and handed Anton a sticky note. "You aren't complaining about Christmas decorations again, are you?"

"Me? Of course not."

She smiled. "That's good. At my house, we leave them up until the middle of January."

He shook his head. "I took my tree down on Christmas evening."

I placed a dessert on a platter. "I love the feeling of Christmastime."

Jett came in the back door. "Hello, everyone." He wiped his snowy boots on the mat and took off his coat. "I just heard back from Detective Madson."

José turned from what he was cooking. "What did he say?"

"They found plenty of evidence pointing to Wayne. He's admitted to everything. He even left the note in his room to make it look like someone was threatening him.

He had Danny write all the notes so they weren't in his handwriting.

"Detective Madson said he's going to be evaluated to check his mental health. He's much too pleased with everything. It's almost like he thinks of it all as a movie. He'd been organizing video clips to put on YouTube. He's not happy they won't let him upload them."

"Did you invite Ledford to the party?" I asked.

"Yes. He sounded like he might come."

Anton groaned. "Why would you invite him?"

"He's not as bad as he used to be, and he doesn't have any family around here." If someone had told me that I would invite Ledford to a party when I first met him, I wouldn't have believed it.

Jett looked out the window. "You'll probably have a good turnout. The snow's only lightly falling, and it's supposed to stop within the hour."

I added another dessert to my tray. "Barbra's nervous about driving in this."

"I talked to her today," Jett said. "I'm going to pick her and Opal up and take them home."

"Did you get a new truck?" Anton asked.

"Yep. It looks like the one I used to have. It's black and practical. I'm not trying to be trendy anymore."

I smiled. "Is that why you liked the Cybertruck?"

"I don't know why I liked it. I guess I liked that it was different. Replacing a tire on that thing was expensive. It cost almost as much as my first car."

My tray was full. I handed it to Jett and asked him to take it to the party room. I followed him with a few tablecloths. I wasn't usually a tablecloth person, but I found some cheap green and red cloths that'd make it all look more Christmassy.

Jett set the desserts on the table and helped me put the tablecloths on. I had cute reindeer decorations that I'd found at a craft shop in Wichita for the centerpieces.

Boyd came in and scanned the room. "What's José cooking? It smells great in here."

"Turkey and potatoes."

"And knowing José, I bet there are a bunch of sides."

I nodded. "It looks like Thanksgiving in the kitchen, not Christmas."

"I took Creepers on a walk."

"He hates the snow."

"He's getting used to it. Of course, I carried him most of the way. I wish I could take Creepers and Conan on walks at the same time."

Jett looked up from where he was straightening a tablecloth. "Have you tried?"

"Only once. That was enough. Conan wants to go fast, and Creepers wants to stop and watch everyone we pass.

I ended up holding Creepers while Conan took us on a walk."

I smiled. Conan wasn't big enough to pull anyone around. He was smaller than Creepers.

"Do you need any help?" Boyd asked.

"I think we're almost ready."

"Who did you invite?"

"Jett's parents. All of my Zumba class and everyone in Barbra's book club. Of course, most of those are the same people. Then there are a few diner regulars and everyone who works here."

Jett finished straightening the table. "I'd better go get Barbra and Opal. I'll be back in about thirty minutes."

I spent the last half hour putting the final touches on the room. By the time the diner closed, the room looked perfect.

José and Anton brought out the food, and Livy greeted people at the door. I wasn't sure people would want to celebrate Christmas after it was over, but the room was full. I'd wanted everything to be low-key. Just a bunch of friends eating and talking together. I stood watching everyone. I hoped they had fun.

José let everyone know it was time to eat, and people filed over to the food table.

"Are you going to sit?" Jett asked me. "You're hovering."

"I'm nervous for some reason."

"Don't be. It's perfect."

It wasn't the food or the turnout. Maybe it was the fact that, for once, everything felt exactly right. That was its own kind of scary.

Jett led me to a chair he'd saved for me.

"Can I get everyone's attention?" Barbra said loudly. "Keep getting food, but listen. Book club is picking new books for next year. A lot of you already belong, but some of you don't. If you want to sign up, come talk to me. If you have any suggestions for books, shout them out and I'll put them on a list."

"*Of Mice and Men!*" Boyd called out. He was at the table, piling potatoes onto his plate.

Barbra wrinkled her nose. "I hate that book. It's depressing."

"I've never read it," Boyd admitted. "I've always wanted to."

"You complain anytime there's a sad ending," Barbra said. "You don't want that one."

"I don't want to read anything that was ever required to be read in school," Opal said. "I swear, teachers only want to make kids read depressing or boring books. If they want kids to love to read, they should read suitable books."

Boyd grinned. "What makes them suitable, and who gets to decide?"

"Kids should get to read things that are popular to their generation. Not things that were written hundreds of years ago. That's why kids hate reading. They don't relate.

You find me a kid who hates reading, and I'll find their interest and get them a book they love."

I shared a smile with Jett.

Barbra ran a hand through her purple hair. "But kids need to learn about the classics."

"Why? Because someone says so. I'm not saying they should never read classics. Just start them off on things they enjoy. Then they become strong readers and can handle all that boring stuff."

"I'm not sure I agree."

Opal rolled her eyes. "You show me a fifth-grade class reading *Harry Potter* and another one reading *The Sign of the Beaver*. I'll tell you what. One class will be happy, and one will be bored."

Boyd shook his head. "Since this is for a book club and not an elementary school, I don't think this conversation applies."

José smiled. "It does if Opal's trying to tell you she wants to read *Harry Potter*."

"I've never read it," Boyd said. "I'd be willing."

Barbra got a few more suggestions, but the conversation quickly died when everyone began eating. Once everyone was sitting, I went and got food with Jett. His parents had decided not to come because of the snow. I was a little relieved. I loved Jett's parents, but I was tired, and Carol would want to talk about the wedding. I'd rather eat and talk about meaningless things right now.

"You can come back for seconds," I teased Jett. "All your food is getting mixed." The pile on his plate was massive.

"I like it that way."

I smirked. "You forgot the vegetables."

He grinned. "Dang it. There's just not enough room on my plate."

"You could add a scoop of green beans on top."

"Why would anyone do that?"

"To be healthy?"

"Maybe later. Oh wait. Later is dessert. I can't have everything."

I shook my head in fake disappointment. "Hey, look," I whispered excitedly. "Jane and Ledford are sitting together."

"You shouldn't get your hopes up. Jane doesn't know many people in town, and no one wants to sit by Ledford. They're together by default."

"So I can't count it as a date?"

He laughed. "Not at all. Not unless he drove her here."

"He might have."

"I doubt it."

"I wonder how I can ask without sounding suspicious."

"Let it go, Ivs. They aren't together."

I took my plate and set it on the table, then walked over to Jane and Ledford. "Hello. I'm glad you two could come."

"This is great," Jane said. "You have great cooks here."

"They are pretty great. Did you drive here?"

"No. I walked from the sheriff's office."

"That will be a cold, dark walk home."

"Jane's tough," Jett said, coming up next to me. "I doubt she's scared of the dark."

"I'm sure we could find someone to drive you back when you're ready."

Jett's eyes sparkled. "I can, if you want a ride."

"No, I like walking in the dark. It's relaxing."

"I'll walk back with you," Ledford offered.

I shot Jett a victory smile.

"Sure," Jane said. "I don't mind protecting you."

Ledford chuckled.

"Well, we'll let you eat," I said, going back to my place.

Jett sat by me and leaned closer. "That's not a date," he whispered.

"It's a step in the right direction."

He winked. "If you say so. You might as well accept that you're going to lose and end up taking care of the animals."

"Never." I ate my turkey and listened to Bing Crosby sing "Have Yourself a Merry Little Christmas." Creepers crawled around my feet. Christmas was over, but somehow, it still felt like a beginning.

When people started leaving, I stood by the door saying goodbye to everyone. The snow was falling lightly, and the vast Kansas sky seemed to go on forever. The snow made everything appear lighter than usual at this time.

Ledford and Jane left together, but they didn't seem any more chatty than usual. Jett might be right. I should probably give up on my hopes for anything happening with them.

After everyone was gone and the diner was cleaned, Jett walked me up to my apartment.

"I fixed your place," he said as I unlocked the door.

"Fixed it? What was wrong?" I walked inside and flipped on the lights. Creepers jumped out of my arms and ran down the hall.

He took my hand and led me to the archway that went into the kitchen. A fresh sprig of mistletoe hung from the arch.

"Oh, I see," I said, putting my hands at the back of his neck. "You did fix it."

"That's one decoration people should leave up all year long."

"But it looks real. It'll die."

"Then let's make sure we don't waste it."

I leaned into Jett's kiss, grateful for the quiet moment. Outside, the snow kept falling, soft and silent. The case was over. The mystery was solved. But best of all, I was exactly where I wanted to be.

Creamy Homemade Eggnog

Ingredients

3 large eggs, plus 2 egg yolks

¾ cup sugar

Pinch of kosher salt

3 ½ cups whole milk

1 ½ cups heavy cream, divided

1 teaspoon pure vanilla extract

¼ teaspoon freshly ground nutmeg, plus extra for sprinkling

sprinkle of cinnamon (optional)

Instructions

In a medium bowl, whisk together the eggs, egg yolks, sugar, and a pinch of salt until smooth.

In a medium saucepan, heat the milk and ¾ cup of the cream over medium heat until steaming, then remove from the heat.

Slowly whisk about 1 cup of the hot milk mixture into the egg mixture to temper it, then pour everything back into the saucepan.

Return the pan to medium heat and cook, stirring constantly with a wooden spoon, until the mixture thickens enough to coat the back of the spoon and reaches 165°F—about 5 minutes.

Remove from the heat and stir in the vanilla and nutmeg. Strain through a fine mesh sieve into a clean bowl. Let cool at room temperature for about 1 hour, then refrigerate until thoroughly chilled (at least 2 hours, or up to 3 days).

When ready to serve, whip the remaining ¾ cup cream to medium peaks. While whisking, slowly pour in the chilled eggnog base. The finished eggnog should be creamy and thicker than heavy cream.

Serve cold, with a sprinkle of nutmeg or cinnamon.

Also By Kristy Dixon

<u>Cozy Mystery</u>
Murder With a Side of Bacon
Murder With a Hint of Cinnamon
Murder With a Fudge Brownie to Go
Murder With a Splash of Vanilla
Murder With a Drizzle of Syrup
Murder With a Slice of Pie
Murder With a Swirl of Blueberry
Murder With a Bite of Biscotti
Suite Lies and Alibis
Not So Suite Caroline

A Suite Case of Murder
Peril Among the Pansies
Murder Among the Moonflowers

<u>Young Adult</u>
The Silver Eclipse (3 books)
The Amethyst Crown
More Than Once Upon a Time
Trapped In Once Upon a Time
The Beginning of Once Upon a Time
Riviand Lost (5 books)

<u>Coming Soon!</u>
Riddles Among the Roses

About the Author

Kristy Dixon started writing stories at age seven and never stopped. These days, she writes cozy mysteries full of quirky characters, small-town charm, and the occasional dead body. She also writes YA novels when the teens in her head get too loud to ignore. Kristy lives with her husband, kids, one spoiled cat, and a flock of chickens who think they run the place. When she's not writing or wrangling her crew, she's likely playing board games, plotting murders (fictional, of course), or dreaming about cookies.